THE NATURE LOVER'S GUIDE TO SURVIVAL

SHIRLEY LALRINFELI

The characters and events portrayed in this book are fictitious. Any similarity to real persons, living or dead, is coincidental and not intended by the author.

ISBN: 978-81-990651-9-2

First Edition 2025

For Popo, who taught me to believe in magical beings

ONE

It was in September that Puia somehow decided that he was tired of his life. It wasn't a decision that he took because of some major mishap. It was rather a series of unfortunate events that somehow ended in a death wish. He stopped coming to school, rarely attended classes, and when he did he often got kicked out for doodling or daydreaming. He drank. A lot. And I guess a seventeen-year-old is not supposed to have all these bottles of alcohol in his room, but he did and he knew where to fill up his stock. Presumably from his dad's.

I wanted him to stop. I tried almost all the behavioural modification techniques that they have come up with to stop addictions. I talked to him about repressed feelings and childhood trauma and everything I could find on the internet. It just didn't work. He wouldn't stop, and I couldn't force it upon him either.

Puia didn't get any better than he was when all of this first started. It didn't help matters much that Anu and Apa were extremely cautious about my hanging out with him, so we met up for nothing more than a few hours every week just to catch up on things. There are a lot of things to catch up on when you've known someone for ten years and they sort of evaporate into thin air, like their whole presence in your life was all just this hazy dream or something.

Puia was the "got his nose in my business but also both hands on my back" friend. The substitute for a big brother, my fellow treasure-hunter and mystery-seeker. A stargazer and moon-watcher every now and then when he fancied becoming one, and always, always a story-appreciator. Now he was light acid rain sprinkling its cold mist on your skin, on the verge of exploding into a downpour.

A usual day in our lives was now markedly different. We talked less, possibly because of the fact that he disliked company (but I constantly imposed it upon him anyway).

I supposedly had Borderline Personality Disorder as a psychiatrist had concluded that I did, so I had to take medication for my supposed depression which I was sure was only sleeplessness disguised as a monster lurking in the dark, but then no one really listened. Anu and Apa insisted that I chit chat with my therapist Pa Terema every week, braving the storm. Because I was a warrior, we come from warrior stock, don't you ever forget that, young woman, that you are a fighter of the greatest physical-and-mental-strength kind, and you should never let that memory slip like a cartoon character slipping on banana peel. Pa

Terema would ask me all these questions about emotions and feelings and all sorts of mumbo jumbo. Then, seeing that I wasn't cooperating, he would sigh and go into a long lecture on the juicy site-of-origin-of-all-rumours that was teenage depression and how I must never give in to the big bad monster of mood disorders and brain chemicals gone awry, some racing at the speed of F1 vehicles while some preferred to laze about in the vacuity of my brain. He was okay, except that I didn't want to tell any strange-looking man that I had dreamt about big gnarly hands clawing at me, nails digging into me, or that I had panic attacks whenever I left for school. These secrets were better left unsaid, leaving them as thoughts that come before words do, before language can expose them.

And then there were the people whom you could share the most amazingly embarrassing secrets with but who won't ever judge you. Puia was one of those very few and fine people. And I knew for sure he would never betray my trust.

It was on a frost-bitten Monday morning in November that Puia came into my room, microscopically thin red lines in his eyes, hair a mess, like he had been caught in a storm and had just narrowly escaped with only his Iron Maiden hoodie to give him what little protection it could. He stank of stale alcohol. Like it would ever surprise me. He crouched by my bed, his head buried in his hands, and I could hear the tick-tock of the clock as the seconds passed by, then a whole minute. I thought his hoodie was black when he came in. When I looked closer, I noticed it had the faint grey of twilight, the colour of a nesting place where birds would flock for food and company, the shade of a safe hiding place. I stepped in on his daydreaming.

"Are you okay?"

"Yeah. Just drowsy."

"Let's go up to the tower."

"Right now? It's too cold up there."

"All the better. Besides, there's something I've been meaning to show you."

We took a ten-minute walk to the water tower, which had an indubitably rich and colourful history, needless to say, what with the badly painted graffiti of Bon Jovi lyrics symbolic of the coming of age of half the town's teen population. We climbed up the ladder and upon reaching the top, took a seat at the same spot where we usually sat, right at the edge of the tower overlooking a large part of the Falkland area, at the point where the cold wind coming from the south hits your face. We were guarded only by a few widely spaced bars. Aizawl in all its splendid entirety of wooden houses on stilts and large concrete buildings rose up on the hills opposite ours. A concrete mass built on the humble bamboo of its ancestors.

From where I sat, I could see them. The family of pigeons that nested in the tin water collector of the building next to the tower. The parents were feeding their young, bringing them worms and insects. I nudged Puia and pointed in their direction, and he mumbled something and I can't remember what he had said, but when I look back on that day, I always remember how I wanted to be like those birds, to be so free that nothing in the known physical world would ever stop me from taking flight to whatever destination I wanted to reach. A shackle-free existence surrounded by white morning mist and jasmine petals that grew right next door lulling me to sleep and below me tall grass, making the sound of drizzle when the wind blew at it.

I wanted freedom, and not of the kind where you're free to wear make-up. Something more, something long-lasting.

I told Puia that this family of birds was the closest thing to perfection that I had ever seen, and he agreed. It was terribly windy that day. Dust collected on my lips and my cheeks. Temperatures had dropped a few days before and still hadn't risen.

He sat beside me, staring into the vast expanse ahead, his face unreadable, his eyes a deep dark black.

"Puia."

He turned in my direction.

"What's going on? You're not yourself. You haven't been yourself for a while now."

"What do you mean?"

"I don't know, I mean, you've changed."

"Oh? I didn't realise."

"Are you sure you're okay?"

He let out a long heavy sigh.

"Amawi, I don't know about anything anymore. I'm so tired of everything. I'm so wasted most of the time, it doesn't matter what I try to do. I can't get anything done and it doesn't make any difference to my family because they're never around anyway. It's just U Seni, and she's away in college now. Tell me, what can I do? What should I do?"

"You can't just waste away like this, Puia."

"Yeah, that's news."

"You just, I don't know, you need to try. You just try, and it doesn't matter if things don't work out. You just need to try a bit."

"I do try my best to survive, alright? So hard sometimes. You don't know how hard."

He picked up a pebble and flung it to the field below us. I wanted to scream at the top of my lungs, to the furthest corner that my voice would carry me, and yell at whatever obtrusive pesky little thing lay in my path.

Puia and I walked home and I went to church in the evening with my friends, but I couldn't get him out of my mind, and through all the hymns that we sang and all through the sermon, I kept going back to him and the sun falling on his dark brown hair as he spoke to me and how his hoodie was a sinister black, and his eyes sad and lonely, and it made me so sad inside to think about it. I tried to suppress it, but there's something about feelings that won't let themselves be suppressed and they will fight their way out to be seen, and felt, and heard, and I just couldn't take it any longer. I shouted inside, the loudest scream that I could have allowed myself to scream, like a sound that hasn't materialised into measurable decibels, and screamed some more in pure emotion, untainted by the acoustics of physical space and away from nosy pesky acquaintances that spread drama like it was the news, and it was such a sad thing to think about.

That was the first time Puia told me about how he really felt, although I'd always sensed it, and whenever I look back on that day, all I remember is the water tower and the heavy wind blowing at us as our legs dangled over the ledge, and how his black eyes looked listless even in the bright of the morning, and the family of pigeons chirping beneath us.

***

I escape to different places, new places, when I need a break from things. So that night I went to the woods and walked through the thick trees and into the hollows where I'd always go. There I found white lilies, the kind that I love. I also found pink and red ones erupting out of the ground from green bulbs. At the mouth of the spring was a white daisy and I thought to myself how I wanted it to be of an altogether new shade, something different, maybe the colour of ocean reefs, majestically blue, with what looked like strips of verdant fields running through it.

I saw it in my mind's eye, a new world filled with lilies and daisies that are of entirely new patterns and colours, and fields that have what seem to be fountains of water gushing through them, flowing upwards in defiance of gravity and spraying water on my face. I saw myself catching droplets with my tongue, tiny droplets the colour of rain-bearing clouds and some the shade of deep, majestic oceans. This was a place where water had all sorts of different shades and flowers reinvented themselves and transfigured into shapes with different hues and textures, and where black earth is now the colour of fancy, iridescent gold dust.

I knew I had to come here again and again. It was a necessity, almost.

I wanted to be there with only my thoughts to keep me company, and maybe see if I could live for eternal time here, to explore the possibilities that this new world held, and not keep myself chained up inside this claustrophobic, damp pigeonhole, because that wouldn't do at all, not when we had the whole world ahead of us.

And what I saw there was a drop of gold emanating from the clouds. But the next instant I saw it again. My heart raced. My hand turned cold and damp. I saw a strong calloused hand grabbing me by the wrist, and it tightened its grip on me, pulling me towards a darkness I could not fathom, and I shouted for it to let me go.

I blinked. The blue lights shone above my bed. Comforting, if not in anything else, at least in their familiarity, and I let out a long sigh. I couldn't erase the image from my mind's eye. It was so powerful and consuming, and all I wanted was to feel safe and protected.

I climbed out of bed, slipped into a hoodie and walked downstairs to the living room. Anu was still up watching a documentary on Nat Geo.

"You're up late," she said.

"I couldn't sleep." She made space for me on the sofa. I slipped in next to her.

"Well you're in luck because look what's airing. A documentary on the food habits of sloths. If that doesn't make you sleepy, I don't know what will."

"Why on earth are you watching this?"

She smiled. "Hey, it was either this or a video of a hippopotamus bathing."

"Isn't there anything better?"

"Apparently the rest of the channels air only PG 13 shows past midnight."

"I'm sixteen."

"Just three years older than thirteen."

I rolled my eyes.

"Oi Anu, em em a. You're too much."

She burst out laughing.

"I'm the parent here. No buts."

"Okay, okay. So I guess we'll just watch a sloth eating his way through an insurmountable quantity of food. What more could I ask for?"

"That's right."

After a moment's pause, I told her. "Nu, I saw it again. It was only a hand that I saw this time, but I got so scared."

"Amawi, Amawi. I'm so sorry Bawihte. It's gonna be fine." She kissed me on my right cheek. I felt safe sitting there with her, the monotonous music on TV giving calming rhythm to my flustered breathing.

"Have I told you the story about the time I went to Champhai for a youth congress?"

No she hadn't.

It had been a long trip, she said, some seven hours in a rattling bus that broke down every hour sputtering and choking on its fumes. When they'd finally reached it was already five in the evening. The service was supposed to start at six. She and her friends were staying at the home of a second cousin who was working at a school there with her husband. They'd washed up and quickly gotten ready for church. On their way up a cobbled and rugged path with no streetlights (their torchlight battery had run out), her friend had lost her balance when she stepped on a log lying in the middle of the road and had fallen into a pig trough. She was drenched in mouldy pig feed that was days old. The second church bell was ringing. Someone would already be at the pulpit welcoming the congregation, reading a Bible verse, and praying for blessings. They had no time to go back and change. She grumbled and rained curses on the frightened pigs, now snorting because they'd smelled food, and this angered her all the more. She was supposed to sing in a trio with Anu and another friend, but it had ended up being a duet where Anu's friend sang way off key in front of thousands of people, because apparently the friend who had had the mishap was the best singer among them. They'd been careful to carry an extra pair of batteries from that night on.

Anu always had the most embarrassing anecdotes up her sleeves, stories revolving around her days in college. They must have been infuriating in the heat of the moment, but they brought a smile to our faces when seen in retrospect. She could have filled quite a large library with them, I reckon.

TWO

It was winter in no time and the streets had lights and Santas and mangers with cardboard cut-outs of Baby Jesus, Mary and Joseph, and the three wise men. We decided to go for a walk around Aizawl on the evening of the 23rd, Puia and I and some friends from school.

John pointed to a star at the top of a pole and said that it looked like someone staring at him. We told him he was being paranoid, but he insisted that it did. There was a street lined with lanterns on all sides and it looked like something out of an anime episode. It was beautiful to look at the light seeping through the holes and it seemed like they were going to float into space any minute now. They looked magical and almost like air because the paper was so thin and see-through. It was white and light shone through it.

There were families with small kids running around, impatiently waiting for their turn on the sleigh, some posing for pictures with a jolly Santa who held out his cap for donations for a children's charity. Couples walking together, arm in arm, and groups of friends on break from school and college. I could almost sense snowflakes falling on my tongue but there weren't any. It was always too warm for that and I wished it wasn't. I wished for a soft layer of white covering the road and the reindeer and the straw huts.

I told Faktei this and she laughed. She said it would never snow in Aizawl. It was always too warm for that, but that was fine. It was still lovely with the off-white lanterns and the reindeer covered in cotton wool.

We walked all the way to the edge of town and John and Faktei took a picture together under a particularly lovely banner welcoming the season. He had his arms around her and I wondered what that would feel like, loving someone in that sort of way. A rush of visible happiness at loving and being loved, maybe a bit of nerves. I always wondered…

There was that guy in class eight who was in the basketball team. He was two years my senior. I never got to know his name. He would walk past me on our way home from school. The closest I got to talking to him was saying thank you when I dropped a book and he'd picked it up for me. There was no eye contact, no blushing, like you see in the movies. He smiled at me and ran to catch up with his friends.

Movies make you think you're supposed to find the love of your life in high school. The nerd and the jock. The Straight A student and the emo punk rocker straight out of a magazine cover. But fairy-tale romances are only for the big screen. It runs cold and freezes here. It's terrible to think about it, that the sun can turn into frost. Cupid running out of arrows. What a story that would be.

But then again, what would I know?

Chhanchhani told me that John was seeing someone else behind Faktei's back, and she was in college and was popular too with the guys. Chhanchhani had had a secret crush on him for months now and she would start any rumour just to get them to break up. She looked pained seeing them together and I almost felt sad for her, that she would lie and hurt people to get her way.

Annoyed, I almost wanted to float into the bright night above us and dance among the warm rays of light and catch falling snowflakes.

I looked over at Puia and he was smiling at me. A smile that said he noticed me daydreaming and he would, I imagined, come to explore this new place with me.

I called him over and he said, for the first time, that I looked pretty. I smiled.

And for the first time in months, he looked glad.

I smiled at him and held his hand and gave it a tight squeeze.

And there we were together, the two of us and no one else, floating in the moonlit sky, snowflakes dripping around us. I caught one on my tongue and let a few more fall on me. The sky was alive with white frost.

I saw John and Faktei and Chhanchhani walking towards me as I went back to my overwhelming reality, and it was like I had never left. It was so difficult to be back here. I imagined yellow eyes glaring at me, ghoulish fiends with green scaly skin prancing around in the darkness, a bulb of neon light a few feet away from where I stood. I closed my eyes and let it take over my senses for a while. I took a deep breath, trying to calm down.

The snow would not stop falling, I imagined, and we walked home through lamplit streets, under lanterns blowing in the wind, through dark lanes to warm blankets and sleepless nights.

The moon peeped at us through dark clouds and would disappear seconds later into melancholy shadows drenched in fog, but all I saw was a blanket of snow piling over me and at last, almost suffocating me. I closed my eyes again and thought of a field, green and yellow, where flowers slept soundly with smiles playing at their corners, and woke up to the call of the morning sun for another day.

In dreams, I saw my friends walking ahead of me in this ocean of lavender and peaches and faded greens, knee-deep now, and seconds later I could see they were covered to the waist. I thought it looked lovely, to wade in a sea of petals and I smiled to myself when I thought that we would go to such a place one of these days.

***

4th of January and we did go, to a small village about 60 km from Aizawl. That morning I grumbled my way into the car while Apa was at the driver's seat telling me to be a sport, we will reach in less than two hours, there wasn't any need to complain, and we hardly ever get any time together as a family except during holidays and I shouldn't spoil this happy family trip. There was no telling when we would be able to plan another trip, so I should stop my endless grumbling and not let it escape my lips. So that was that, and Anu climbed into the front seat and we said a small prayer, thanking God for this opportunity and asking for his protection and blessings, and we started our two-hour-long journey through winding lanes that sent our stomachs wobbling and our heads topsy-turvy.

But one hour into the trip with soft music drifting from the radio and overgrown brambles wandering onto the highway, and I was already ecstatic to be here. I felt the music around me, overwhelming in its melodious highs and lows, and I saw golden leaves dropping one by one onto the grass below. I tasted the warm sun on my tongue as the wind blew stray strands of hair across my face.

"Your mom and I have been looking forward to this weekend, just to get away from Aizawl. It's so congested these days with traffic and buildings shooting up like grass."

"It's not like the old days anymore. You can't sleep without a truck rumbling outside your window every five minutes. The holiday season is the worst."

"It's so much more quiet here," I said.

"And we wanted to give you a holiday before the final exams. After that you'll be in your final year of school and you'll have board exams to prepare for, and then your entrance exams," Apa said.

It was always about exams and studies with them, as though school could prepare me for a rich and glorious future, like it wasn't just a series of tests to quantify our memory, but really credible tests of intellect.

We reached after a punctured tyre and another twenty minutes on the dusty, winding roads of Mizoram but thankfully without any serious hiccups. Apa parked the car on the side of the road and we walked twenty metres to a pond teeming with tadpoles, where weeds sprang up and swayed in the current. As I dipped my feet into the sparkling water I saw ten thousand tadpoles encircling me and nibbling on my skin. In a matter of seconds I saw green glossy boils erupting on my toes and then on the soles of my feet and I shivered at the thought but laughed inside to think that I would really turn into a frog if tadpoles bit my skin. The thought was farfetched and almost like a story made for Superheroes, not everyday sixteen-year olds like me, and I laughed to think about it.

I saw Anu seated on an elevation jutting out from the rocky banks and picking up smooth and flat stones to use as pumice. It felt wonderful seeing her, the sun making her hair glisten and stray strands falling on her cheeks, and to see Apa inspecting the bushes around us with hunter-like acuity on the lookout for danger.

I took out my lace handkerchief, dipped it in the water, and tadpoles swam towards it. I lifted them up to the surface and saw their slimy skin under the bright sunlight. They swam in circles, the little creatures that I saw nibbling on my toes and my ankles, and I smiled to think how tiny they really were, that they won't have any venom to turn me into one of them, even if they could, and I laughed again at the thought. Hey there, big guy, I said to the largest of them, the most well-fed, and it felt weird talking to it when I knew it couldn't hear me. I released all of them into the pond and they swam in circles again, like that was what they were made for.

Anu said that the sun was particularly bright that day and we were lucky that it didn't rain. It often rained in January, a short burst of thunder and lightning that had been kept at bay during the winter, saving itself for the one perfect January day on which to unveil itself and burst forth. We gathered our tiffin and water bottles from the car and walked the five kilometres to the top of the sprawling hills. The hillside was near dry and there was very little vegetation except for a few grasses springing up in spite of the tremendous dearth of moisture. Dead leaves rustled under our boots with every step that we took. We saw a few stray blossoms every two feet or so, some white and some lavender, tender and withering blooms that told us that there was little life here.

Anu noticed a good spot to set up our stuff, under a dying tree that offered very little shade, but the air was cold, almost, especially at the hilltop, and a little sun was harmless. I pulled out a blanket from my bag and spread it on a level piece of ground. Apa placed our lunch baskets on top of it. It felt like we had absolute respite here and it was freeing, like a moment of inspired euphoria, if there is such a thing, and I took it in as salt takes in water.

We played a game of rock paper scissors, then Monopoly and finally Scrabble, and Apa tried to invent the words "jutleer" to mean a precipice which looks like it has hollows for eyes. The other words were "husdry" which is short for husbandry, as in animal husbandry, (like one syllable made such a huge difference), and "shanimangtre," an expression that supposedly meant that you're craving some rasmalai.

“You always do that whenever we play Scrabble,” Anu complained. “It’s really annoying.”

“Those are the dumbest words ever invented,” I said.

Sometimes Apa would even use them in a sentence way after a game was over, and Anu and I would look at him with quizzical eyes, wondering if we had heard him right. When he was done tormenting us, he would remind us of so and so Scrabble game and tell us to call up the people at Oxford English Dictionary to remind them to add it to the latest edition, that whenever he uses it, he wouldn't have to explain it to us.

Anu would roll her eyes in exasperation like she did now and say that she had had enough of word-inventing for a day. She told us of how a colleague of hers had told her to her face yesterday that women shouldn't be allowed to hold important jobs because they always need maternity leave and they take days off complaining about period cramps. But I was a single child so she only took a maternity leave once, and I don't remember her taking a day off complaining about cramps no matter how painful it looked, and I said that it was disgusting to talk to a woman that way. Like her pain doesn't count because it is a part of her monthly cycle, because it is the sort of pain that men can’t see. And even if she did take days off because of period cramps, she was entitled to take days off whenever she wanted to. She was at liberty to do so.

Anu shook her head and said that the environment at her workplace was terrible. Her colleagues smoked in their cubicles, sometimes right in front of a no-smoking sign, and cigarette puffs would fill their room. It was no place to work in for the next twenty years, I thought. It would ruin her health. But Apa couldn't ask her to resign because we needed a steady income. Our electronics repair shop had been stagnant for a few months now and we had to pay off loans. House rent was sky high in the town centre where we had our shop and it was always risky starting a business in a town with a population of just three lakhs, where businesses and shops sprang up like clustered gooseberries.

But my parents always said that one, we had warrior blood boiling in our veins telling us not to give in. Two, to fight is to get the work done even if we don't see the results immediately. Three, that there is dignity even in losing as long as we get our work done. Four, there is no such thing as losing, only unexpected results, and a tremendous level of patience is developed in waiting for the ground to sprout the first signs of greenery.

I always told them three and four contradicted each other but they said I should think more along the lines of "never giving up," and that suited me just fine.

The sky was spotted with white clouds that looked like fleece, ones which reminded me of cotton wool without a hint of the smell of disinfectants, nature untarnished by disease and illness, and it felt wonderful to see them floating, unhurriedly, towards the south-eastern sky. I walked to the hilltop and spread out below me was a sprawling field of dried grass just like the ones we had here. It would have looked wonderful in the monsoon and rain would have made it greener but here it was no more than a dry cheerless heath.

I took a deep breath and imagined that it looked a bit livelier than it did now, like I was watering the grassy hills myself.

Huts and dried grass soaking in the winter dew, taking in water vapour from the atmosphere, trees almost falling to the ground under the weight of heavy winds, grasslands and how they can make you feel and see the yet unexperienced—it seemed magical to my young mind.

***

It is 3:30 in the morning and I wake up sweaty from a dream. I see him again, not just his hands but his face too. A square face with a thin moustache and beady eyes. He is walking towards me and I try to run but I can't move my feet. I try to shout for help but it comes out muffled and throaty. I try to ward him off but he has my arms clenched in his rough hands.

I shout and wake up before I see anything else.

I say a small prayer to calm myself down. The fairy lights are dangling above me but I am dazed. I can't see a thing. My heart is racing still and it is all I can do to keep from breaking down.

THREE

A few days later, Puia and I met up for the weekend. A Labrador pup dressed in a pumpkin suit came running towards us, his tail wagging in excitement. When the pup had gone back to his owner, Puia, his head bent down, observed his bowl of sundae like it was fake lava erupting from the volcanoes that we made for science projects back in primary school.

"What's wrong?" I asked in characteristically tactless fashion.

"It's my dad. He comes home drunk every night…What on earth is wrong with him? And my mom couldn't care less about him."

"I hope things get better, Puia."

"Yeah. It feels pointless sometimes."

I nodded that I understood. I didn't really, although I wanted to.

"What's the point, Amawi. It doesn't get better. It has not gotten better in years now," he said, playing with his now melted ice cream, making circles in his bowl. "It would be easier to just let go of it all, because whatever I try, I don't know if it's going to work. And you know something else? It always gets worse. Yeah. Every time."

"Puia," I said. I was silent for a long time before I finally managed to say something. Words get stuck somewhere in your thoughts and decide to abandon you when you need them the most. "I think of the same things that you think about. The truth is, I don't know if it gets better or if it just falls apart all the time. But maybe this is just one small fraction of your life—the things that weigh you down. Your life is so much bigger than that. And maybe you're stuck in a terrible situation now, but it won't always be like that, right? I mean, there's always so much to live for."

I hated my sentimentality. I sounded like I was trying to inject some concoction labelled "happiness" in gaudy yellow lettering into the dark nihilistic veins of a seventeen-year-old without so much as an attempt at empathy. Stupid stupid stupid.

He sat back in his chair and gazed at the empty space in front of him. His eyes were full of distant places and lonely people. I could not discern what or who even after years of secrets being shared between us. He was a distant nebula, and I was a dull meteor that wandered aimlessly. I couldn't help him, try as I may. I couldn't even help myself.

"Yeah, you're right. You say the smartest things every once in a while, though not very often," he said, coming back to the situation at hand.

"Yeah, and this is one of those times, apparently," I said.

"Most of the time, you speak the most nonsensical things. I have to remind myself that you are Lalnunmawii My Best Friend and not an Extra-Terrestrial who is having a hard time adjusting to life here on Earth."

***

The night of the farewell party we had planned for our seniors arrived. It was at this eighties themed retro club in Chanmari, with glaring disco lights hanging from the ceiling and party music booming everywhere. All our seniors were pretty wasted and so were my classmates. I was getting tired of all the noise and went to the balcony and sat there, the breeze blowing softly on my face and my neck. The rich warm scent of jasmines floated across the heavy night air, and it was so soothing, so heavenly, after all that cigarette smoke. And I turned off every thought in my head and took a deep breath and all around me were miles upon miles of flowing grey grass, almost the colour of hay. When I opened my eyes, the sky had darkened. It was twilight. I saw Anu's face in the expanse of the darkening sky. She was smiling at me, and her eyes were the stars. Apa had his arms wrapped around her, and he was gazing at me, almost in a frown, like he was concerned.

At the end of the hallway a guy was running to the toilet, trying to keep himself from puking in front of everyone, and another guy was supporting his girlfriend who could barely walk, and I felt the tall grass brush against my hands as I ran across the field and flew up to the sky to be where my parents were, like I had wings or something. I felt the cold air rush into my lungs and

I breathed out warmth the next second. I saw a silhouetted figure approaching me and sit down next to me. It was Puia.

"Mind if I join you?"

"Not at all."

"What a waste of time, isn't it? They're all idiots," he muttered.

"At least the party is a success."

"Yeah, we threw them one helluva going away party, you know, just to celebrate them not bullying us anymore."

"Uh-huh."

"But you've got to admit, they're so bent on sucking all the juice out of this, I kinda admire them. The way I see it, Amawi, there are two kinds of people in this world. The ones who go after what they want, no matter the cost. They will fight till their very last breath to see that they get what they truly want in life," he said as a matter-of-factly. "Even if that something is getting drunk till you can't even stand straight anymore and you puke all over the car. Then there are people who are too afraid to go after their dreams. They're scared."

"And in which category do you fall?" I asked him.

"The first one, obviously. No questions asked. I don't want to deny myself the pleasure of living every moment to the fullest."

"Yeah. That's an awful cliché. Live every moment to the fullest and everything will be swell and jolly. It's not even possible."

I just didn't believe in it because I had tried to do that every single day and I had always failed. Good and bad must co-exist in this world and so on. Like yin and yang.

"It's not cliché if it's true."

"You're an awful excuse for Hedonism, Puia."

"Aaah I get you. I get you."

"It's just, when you try to escape all of this, your life, everything… I don't know. Don't you think you should confront it, maybe? Can't you try? I mean, at least try." He looked pained and I bit my tongue. "Yeah. Never mind. I'm sorry. What was I thinking?"

"It's alright, I get you loud and clear. Everything is so clear in my head and what you're saying is just so little of what I tell myself."

"I'm sorry."

"Hey, no worries. You're good." He tousled my hair and I felt like an idiot. My mind was in a whirlpool with thoughts from here and there swinging in confusion and making a ruckus.

I told him about the field that I saw and how the colours were changed and lilies were brand new colours. The drive home felt magical—I saw pretty lights everywhere. As I sat on my bed, I remembered how great it felt to be there, and decided to write down a survival plan. I got up, walked over to my desk, and rummaged through my drawer for a notebook, one with a floral cover, which Anu had given me on my fifteenth birthday, and grabbed a pen. I turned on the LED lights above my bed, opened the door to the balcony to let the breeze in, and I turned to the first page.

This is my guide to survival. Immerse yourself in the world of nature overflowing with green and serene beauty, one which is far removed from its man-made counterpart, the universe of brick and concrete jungles and stone walls.

Step One of the Nature Lover's Guide to Survival: The Marshes

Go to the marshes at dusk and you will find glowworms there, fireflies floating above the swamps, turning the scene into something beautiful. Forget everything you've been told about how ferocious the animal kingdom can be. Relearn what it means to be human, so you can live in harmony with nature.

While you're there, breathe in the scent of everything else that is around you, all that is not affected by the stench of the rotting vegetation. As you explore whatever there is to explore, be on the lookout for flowers, especially sea lavenders and marsh rosemary (lilac blue water lilies will do if you can't find anything else), and let them be, a crown on their stems, but bend towards them, go nearer, lean into the petals and take in a breath of their perfume. Think about what it does to you and how you feel light-headed with just one breath, and take a step back to consider if it arouses in you any glimmer of whatever God-given hope you still may have. Take in the sound of the waters breathing with life. Of waters filled to saturation with algae and ferns and detritus, of green terrestrial matter turning into atmospheric matter and breathing new life. Taste the electrifying scent of pure marsh air, undiluted and pungent, as it pulses around you and spills into your eyes, your hair. Breathe it in, allow it to seep into your skin and revitalise all that is dry and dying.

I'd seen pictures like this, where dense air filled the whole frame in a sort of magical way, like vapour became something that could be seen but not with your eyes, a thing that you could experience through your other senses. I always wondered how you could feel it around you when it was humid and if you could see it, almost, if it became even heavier, but not like mist or fog. Something different. It only followed that if you could feel it around you at its most humid, then at one point in time, you should be able to see it too, and maybe smell the carbon dioxide or something if it gets too concentrated in the air around you.

And the next moment there was a wave of carbon dioxide around me and a dense cloud encircling my chest, closing in on me, wrapping its arms around me, and I opened my eyes and my room was bright with cool sky blue lights, my bed was full of books and paint and brushes and my cactus was right where I had left it. Everything was as it was supposed to be, nothing had changed, but I was suffocating as though heavy stones were being thrown at me. Anu must have heard me gasping for air because she rushed into my room.

"What's wrong, Mate?" she said. "Are you okay?"

"I'm fine, just had a long day."

"Are you sure?"

"I'm okay, Nu. Really."

"Did you have a nightmare or something?"

"Sort of. I'm fine, Nu." She looked worried as she stood there in front of me, wringing her hands.

"Well, alright then. I'll leave the windows open to let in some fresh air."

"Thanks."

A five-second pause. She looked worried.

"Amawi, we should see your doctor tomorrow. You have started acting, well, you haven't been yourself lately. You have built up a defence around you, and Pa Terema says it's normal for kids your age to feel a bit of this… this *adolescent angst*, you know, when they're nearing adulthood, but there's a healthy way to express your emotions. You need to build the tools to be more emotionally equipped for your future, and that includes expressing what you feel. We're family, and this is the place to do that."

"Nu, I'm fine. Really."

"Amawi, I know you're not. Look what happened five minutes ago."

"Can I just get some sleep? I'm tired." I shouted into my pillow so she wouldn't hear me, but pillows don't work as great as vacuum, apparently.

"Don't yell at me, young lady. Now get your act together and you will go make an appointment with your doctor tomorrow, do you hear me?"

"Nu, I'm fine. I just had a long day and I'm tired. That's all."

"You don't look fine at all, Amawi. You need a professional to take care of you. Now I won't have any more of this."

"Nu."

"I said enough."

"Okay okay."

"Now go to bed. It's late."

She left the door open a tad bit so that a streak of light fell in from the hallway and lit up my desk and there were tiny elves dancing on it, doing hula hoops with my watch, somersaulting on top of my chemistry book, and climbing on my lamp, and I saw a forest filled with mushrooms where the elves were carving microscopically small spoons out of wood and employing tremendous craftsmanship to make tiny umbrellas. I walked over to my desk, grabbed a book, (I think it was a horribly written murder mystery, I can't remember exactly) and read it under starlight, the brightest I have ever seen.

I could hear my parents in the next room, speaking in hushed tones like they always do when they have something on their minds, and Anu was sniffling and I felt the weight of a thousand boulders and ten thousand oceans surrounding me.

FOUR

So the next day Apa took me to the clinic where a nurse examined me and said that I was as fit as a fiddle, maybe even better, if that was possible, and asked me to go upstairs and wait for my turn. We had to climb up a cramped staircase lined with empty cardboard boxes stacked one on top of the other at odd angles. White *chinai* was smeared on the walls. The waiting room looked more like a small garage. We sat down on a tiny bench. When it was my turn, Apa gave me an encouraging nod and told me that I will get through this whole phase, if only I tried hard enough and listened to the doctor. I got up. The door creaked as I pushed it open and the psychiatrist was sitting on his chair, scrolling through his phone, and without looking up, told me to sit down. He took another scrumptious bite of his *kuhva* and red juice oozed out the side of his lips, and as he put his phone away, asked me what was the matter, and he scribbled on his notepad as I told him my symptoms.

If there are a few things I've learnt about myself, one is that I can't be a lone heroine, like when I build a fortress out of cherry blossoms and sadness, and at the slightest breeze, it crumbles like it never existed at all, not even for a second in time, and all traces of years of labour vanish into darkness. And out of the Nothing that I see in front of me, I pick up frayed petals, and glue them back together and rebuild a Fortress-in-Disarray piece by piece. It is of course fragile, unsteady, but better than nothing.

I heard bits and pieces of what the doctor said, like "your life is precious, you are special" and "whatever your problems may be now, even if they seem heavy and too big for you, as time goes on, you will realise that they're just a speck of dust" and "don't worry your parents, they love you." He said that all that negative energy I have can be toxic if I don't learn to control it, if I don't learn to channel it into something I love to do. "Take time to develop your hobbies. Whenever you feel your thoughts going in the wrong direction, channel them towards the things you like to think about. It might be difficult, but it will come with practice. Think of what gives you joy and run towards it, fight for the good things."

It's funny how I still see myself as a loner disguised as a heroine. Even after everything.

***

Puia said that there was a carnival in town and asked me if I wanted to go. He said that they had fun games, and I felt bored from a long weekend of doing nothing except bingeing on TV so

I said yes. I pulled on a jacket and slipped into my faded Vans. We entered the gates of Lammual and Puia exclaimed, "We don't have much time to waste. The world expects us to burst through its golden gates and fly. Can't keep it waiting."

"Please."

"Hurry up, Amawi. You're always so slow. Don't waste a pleasant evening."

There were these big colourful tents that dotted the open space and large crowds bustling past the displays of games and carousels. I saw men on stilts, vendors with cotton candy of all colours ranging from pink to purple to green, women carrying their babies and their husbands holding their young sons and daughters by the hand so that they wouldn't run away.

Music boomed from speakers that were placed all around us. There was lively Bollywood music that actresses dance to in the movies. There was activity in every corner, small kids running around the carousels and the Ferris wheel and stalls that had tons of tempting games.

"Amawi, let's go ride the Ferris wheel," Puia suggested as we strolled through the sights and attractions.

"I don't know," I said.

"Why not? It'll be fun, come on," he prodded.

"You know I'm scared of heights."

"It won't sting a bit, I promise," he said as he grabbed my hand and pulled me towards the gates of the Ferris wheel.

I yelled at him to let go of my hand, but he only held on tighter and pushed me into the nearest booth.

"Come on, Amawi." He made me sit next to him and held my arms tight so that I had absolutely no way of escaping. "You won't regret it."

We ascended slowly as people filed into the remaining booths, and I froze in my seat, unwilling to look anywhere but straight ahead at the now dimly lit sky. There were all these sounds below us, sounds that slowly faded away as we went higher up. Fireworks were bursting some distance away, blazing in the dark of the night and exploding into a spectrum of colourful hues.

"Amawi, look at the ground," Puia whispered next to me. By now we were forty feet into the air and the ride was starting and all that I could think of was what a free fall would feel like. I dived headfirst into the air that enveloped me, and a thick cloud cushioned my fall. I bounced on it like it was a trampoline and I laughed to think that I had lost my fear of heights. Puia nudged me and I saw the metal bars across my chest and held on tighter, trying not to fall.

"We're really high up, aren't we?" I said.

"Sort of."

"It feels scary but the adrenaline rush feels good. It's been a while since I did something like this."

"I told you, didn't I?"

I summoned up the courage to have a peek at the carnival below us. The lights were magnificent.

"Beautiful, isn't it?" he said.

"Yes, it is," I agreed.

“I told you you wouldn't regret it. I’ve been on these rides hundreds of times but the view never ceases to amaze me. Look to your right.”

I did. The city lights stretched into the distance, extending for miles beyond us. Buildings that had small blocks of white and fluorescent yellow coming out of them rose many storeys above the ground.

To my left, I could see stretches of hills that in the daylight would be dotted with foliage, but right now they were as dark as a black hole.

Aizawl looked different from up here, like a town full of tiny lights glimmering in the dark. It looked prettier. The hills beyond us looked peaceful, as though they were in deep sleep. Things are always more beautiful when you can’t see them clearly.

***

Puia came over the next evening, hair a tangled mess and eyes bloodshot red. He was angry. His eyes always shot on fire whenever he was angry, and he looked like a crisis-gripped sleepwalker who would snap at the slightest disturbance. He paced up and down my room, and had his hands on his face and he cursed repeatedly. I let him be. It was how he dealt best with things, and it wasn’t like I knew what to say to him.

He eventually calmed down.

“This is a mess,” he said, and I asked him what was the matter, and he weighed his options, whether he should report it to a women’s rights organisation or keep things hush hush. I told him it would be better to report the matter, whatever it was, and seek some sort of help, because it had gone on for too long. Once was enough, and this was beyond the limit.

Pa Mawia, Puia's dad, was famous all over the neighbourhood for his temper, and it was fine when it was the occasional rant at a biker who had parked in front of his garage, or a fist shown at a passer-by who spat on the walls of his house. But he would turn violent on Nu Maawmi, Puia's mom. It had happened again this evening. He was drunk. He had left after that. He would be gone for the rest of the week. He always was.

It's funny how Pa Mawia would start doting on her again when he came back.

A monstrosity that defeats the human form, taking over a person's humanity and leaving bruised bones and blood spilt like tears on the floor. It's like the perpetrators are blindfolded and all that they can see in front of them are apparitions of themselves, their worst failings and fears. When they raise the first fist against their victim, and rain the first blow on the Madonna, it's an attempt to kill their ugly parts. The parts they can't live with. The ones that haunt them in nightmares, the ones that follow them into the light, merging with their shadows, a ubiquitous presence. The drunk and disillusioned elephant in the room which they can't seem to shake off. The rash and hot-headed elephant in a crumpled party hat.

One moment cold, hot the very next. That's what domestic violence is, a morphed two-faced thing in hideous garb. Never in an equilibrium, never stable.

We took a lazy stroll around the neighbourhood, watching people with their dogs and kids running and screaming as they played on the streets, a vendor with a bucket full of alu papawr and packets of imported junk food parked in the corner underneath a cherry tree in full bloom. Town buses filled with passengers, taxis waiting for customers, and school children in uniform walking with sagging bags heavy with books. You could hear the chirping of what seemed like an orchestra of crickets. A sure sign that the weather tomorrow would be warm and humid. The setting sun cast pink and orange hues over everything it fell on, over the tin roofs of houses, over the foliage which now had an orange tinge.

We took a seat on a bench that was almost hidden by a thicket and all these Mayflowers.

The sky was almost dark now, with birds cawing and flying back to their nests, and flooding the cloudless sky with their dark silhouettes.

And in a moment the sky was an ethereal pink with what looked like orange marmalade scattered across the expanse, swirling and twirling, orange peel dusted with powdered sugar tied into thin bundles. Silverfish floated across the sky and into the vast unknowns of space, and Puia was sitting beside me, and I pulled at his arm. Like I was the missing link between the sky and him, him and the sky, and I wanted him to see it too, this etheresque limitless singularity, and I pulled him up on his feet, and he could barely lift them, they were so heavy, and I called to him to come, come quickly, as he trudged beside me and grew wings and was lifted up into the limitless oceanic expanse. He smiled for a while, and I only wanted to be that connecting factor, nothing more. Below us there were barely any trees, but there were loaded garbage trucks and a town with too much traffic and too many buildings crammed next to each other like Legos blocks, and I saw ten-foot-tall trees beginning to take root, spreading a network under the tar roads which cracked in the middle.

The stone bench felt heavy under my body. The tree in front of us was growing roots, spreading a network whose tips almost touched the surface of the groundwater below, as leaves sprouted and birds built nests on a safe branch. Blossoms blown in the wind carpeted the stony path below us. This pinkish white, so beautiful and delicate, was stained with brown footprints. Street vendors were packing up, and Puia sat there scrolling through his phone in the midst of this tremendous action, oblivious to the growing of the roots and the falling of a petal on the muddy footpath below us. In a space all his own, uninhabited except for his presence and the occasional passer-by who chanced to walk in on his unguarded thoughts. There was hardly any room for anything else inside his head. It was like a stuffy closet, and I imagined that it would be filled with tattered photographs and muddy footprints. Posters pinned to the walls, almost to the point of saturation, that looking at them fills you with a gnawing sense of unease, an overwhelming sense of imminent destruction. Tiny gnome-like creatures with diabolical eyes hiding under clumps of dust, and all you want to be is that link, that connecting factor, and you don't know how. To bring this disaster into the light and maybe a bit of order, even just a bit, and maybe it will be less of this horrid, unkempt mess. To turn things around and stop a cyclic force that goes back in time, and forward into the future.

FIVE

I woke up the next morning to the sound of horns honking on the street outside my room, but I could still hear birds chirping on the balcony. I decided I was going to have a good day, and I told myself I could pick it up a notch. I was in tiptop shape, as great as any other day, and I knew things were working out. I said a small prayer of thanks and got out of bed. I saw petals falling into a stream and floating on the surface, and I walked towards it. Anu was downstairs making breakfast. I helped her out. The morning news was airing on TV, and scrambled eggs were simmering on the stove. A perfect morning.

Anu smelled faintly of roasted cocoa. She had curly hair, one of the few things I got from her, and it was tied up in a knot. People always said I look more like my grandma though. She died when Anu was in middle school, and the only things I know about her are stories Anu and Pu Thlana told me. We have a few pictures of her too, one a framed photograph of the four of them, Anu wearing her best Sunday clothes and Pu Thlana, his hair covering his forehead, dressed in disco pants (they were all the rave back in those days), and Api looking like a deer caught in headlights, dressed in a puan that looked old and worn, and her hair wild and frizzy, just like mine. She had beautiful eyes and they looked scared in that picture. When I was five, I asked Anu why and she said that Api had never stood in front of a camera before. It was the first family photo that she ever took, and also the last. Things were difficult in those days. Apu played the part of the steadfast husband, although he was feeble and weak after twelve years of a marriage ensnared in the grips of poverty. He had on a tattered jacket and shoes that he had walked miles and miles in. They were parents who had sacrificed blood and sweat for their children.

There weren't any supplies of rice. The rats had eaten everything. It was the period of Mautam and the insurgency and the sky rained down drops of mercury on its own people, its very own flesh and blood, but who aren't as important as other people living under its dominion because well, to be frank, they look different, almost Chinese, and they eat dogs and sometimes even snakes, and what sort of a person does that, shame shame. They needed to be taught a lesson, these good for nothing tribals who think they deserve the same rights as those well-bred high caste chaps. Shame shame. Rain down mercury on their land if they still have the impudence to raise their fists in protest, teach them a lesson they will never forget, tch tch. Barge into their homes and take their women for yourselves and leave them writhing in the dust when you've shown them your fantastic machismo, that's all you have to boast of anyway.

Take all of their provisions, even the smallest quantities, and then hit the woman who tries to resist, because her two children are hungry and her husband is sick and can't go out to the fields. If you're depraved enough, you'll leave them without a mother, to be cared for by an ailing father.

Anu and Pu Thlana grew up handsome and beautiful, kind and strong. They fought for what they had. I told myself I had the strength, the ability, to fight too. Like Anu, like Pu Thlana, like Api, like Apu. It was in my blood to fight. I was born with a sheath and cried the roar of a warrior at birth. I had warrior genes embedded in my cells, pushing me with every ounce of energy that I had to put up a struggle, even if it was as minimal as raising a finger, now was the time for me to fight.

I decided, yet again, and told myself yet again that I was going to have a good day. Any element driving my mind in the other direction would go down as long as I was clothed in battle armour. This family heirloom that I could feel all around me. It filled my every sense and shielded my every thought. I would fight, like Anu told me to every night before I slept, and on every foggy day when everything else was living in the shadows.

All the people in my life had gone through tough stuff and they had made it, limbs intact and everything, a tiny scratch on the shin, a gash in places maybe, but they had made it. And they never made much of a fuss, at least not when I was around, and I wanted them to be especially proud of me, and for me to be a jolly happy-go-lucky young girl. I had to *recuperate*, as the doctor would put it, and start becoming tremendously unbelievably happy.

Step Two of the Nature Lover's Guide to Survival: Deserts

Deserts are tricky places. They're cold one moment, sizzling hot the next and only a few life forms can survive there. But for you, if you're bent on beating this and are willing to break your bones and strain a few muscles for it, it's one of the most crucial stops you'll ever make.

Watch sand dunes getting destroyed to nothing and then recreated into sandy hillocks by the desert wind, as it carries grains of white sand for miles and miles. Make for yourself in the desert a tent to protect you from sandstorms. Pitch it near the first oasis you can find. Let it be a shelter for you away from the sweltering heat of day and a place where you can rest your head awhile, where heartbeats are calmer and thoughts start slowing down. As night approaches and daylight breaks away bit by bit, snuggle up next to your favourite stuffed animal. Allow it to lead you back to ten years ago, as you nervously tug at your sweatshirt. You then clear the brambles in front of you and set them on fire. Find in the desert a cool spring that satiates you, and experience a revivification as you let it drip, drop by drop, onto your skin. And as the cool water envelops you, look up at the skies and remember how the oceans are almost, but not quite, the same hue. How they can be an even deeper blue, a dense oceanic blue. Remind yourself of how they are teeming with life. See in the skies the possibilities that the world around you holds.

Because Anu had braved the storms. When people her age were hopping around in other people's old dilapidated jeeps, music blaring at almost immeasurable volumes, all dolled up in rouge, she was running around town selling knickknacks to earn a few paises here, a few paises there. She would get up at four in the summer, five if the sun was a bit late, and carry buckets to the tuikhur. They had a small barrel at home, and she would fill it to the brim with water. They had a small shed in the garden for a toilet, like most houses back then, and it was always a test of courage to go pottying in the middle of the night. They heard howls and you could just feel the animals prowling right behind you, so close you felt their warm breath tingling your skin, their wet noses just inches away from you, ready to pounce on you any moment now. At four in the morning, Anu would wake up, and roll over on her bed hoping to catch a few more minutes of sleep. It was at the brackish grey light of dawn that she got up, walked fifteen minutes to carry bucketfuls of water, and then got ready for an hour of work before school.

Apu told me a story once of how strong Anu was. One morning a thunderstorm was brewing. The sky turned dark and rumbled—it sounded like the tumbling of empty barrels. Anu had just minutes before left for her morning ritual, selling vegetables neatly packed in an em, trudging under the heavy load. It started raining and Apu went to the corner where he kept his umbrella, walked out into the rain, thinking I must go find Mami or she'll get soaked in this storm (this is so difficult, taking care of two young children with nothing more than a few rupees a month—the burden of making ends meet). The rain is too strong. It beats down so hard on this soft earth. Splashes of mud. Flash floods. She couldn't have gone too far, she left just minutes ago.

He did find her, shivering outside a neighbour's house, drenched, her hands cold and numb, a wet shawl covering her shoulders.

She had caught a bad cold and was sick in bed for three days. Apu didn't let her go out alone after that. He said it was too risky, too dangerous for a young girl such as her and what would he do without her, she was his only daughter. (A copy of her mother, especially around the eyes, and what eyes, just like her mother's—thoughtful, curious, but never those of a cold intellectual, never. Soft and warm, and bright. How a daughter could resemble her mother.)

Apu opened a small shop and Anu would work there after school, and Pu Thlana would go to the Bazaar to get stuff for the shop, and Apu would, on most days, work at the farm, digging the earth and sowing seeds, but the money wasn't great and they could barely make ends meet. They managed to put food on the table, and had just enough for school fees and books. The rest they saved up for the holidays when they would buy gifts for one another. But they were built with the kind of gritty stamina and strength that strangers would perhaps mistake for callous rowdiness. They were giving and generous even with the little that they earned. They believed them to be blessings from God, so they gave to others what they got from the Lord. It was required of them, it was their duty, difficult as it may be at times when what they had barely sufficed. But then again, they were blessed with all the tools to survive deserts and they thrived here too.

They had to. There was no choice but to push on past the derision and scorn of some of their less affable neighbours, to not just turn a deaf ear and a blind eye towards their crude jokes, but also, and this was the difficult part, a forgiving heart that had no anger, resentment or all of that ugly gruesome stuff that can fester inside open wounds. Because it was the more Christian thing to do, do unto others as you would have them do unto you, my Apu would say to his children.

SIX

Puia said that he remembered a painting I did a year ago. A stunted tree in the middle of a vast prairie. He said that he liked it and would much rather hang that in his room than some poster of a rock band. I'm glad that he did, and I'm glad that he said it with sincerity. He jokingly said that he would make it to the front pages of all the famous art magazines if my works were his, because he will have all the connections, people skills and all. I told him he was welcome to steal them, just not under my nose. He told me that my future was to become a stereotypical struggling artist, albeit a content one.

"I'm not enamoured of eating rice and dal for the rest of my life," I told him.

"Just saying," he said. "I wouldn't mind rice and dal as long as I'm passionate about my work. You get cold feet at the most critical moment." And I wondered how this was one such moment, but never mind.

"You are so darn pragmatic. You need to loosen up a bit. What did I tell you, Amawi? There are only two kinds of people in this world and you needn't be so darn uptight all the time. Wait, let me show you something."

He pointed at a stone building that lay uninhabited across the street. It had always been like that from when I was a kid.

"What do you see there?" he asked me.

"A building. And some trees here and there, a few birds perched on the roof," I replied.

"See? You see only what your eyes see. Only the physical. You need to set your imagination free and observe all the possibilities that that old place right there holds. Now, do you see what I see?"

He looked me square in the eyes. I said that I did not.

"I see a yellow house. There's a woman in the garden, watering the plants. She's the wife of a businessman who lives there. They have two young kids, one is seven and the other is all of ten. They are intelligent kids, but sadly the younger one was diagnosed with a heart condition and now she is in and out of hospital. You see that dog there? That's their pet, Rudolf. He's a red-nosed indie. They've had him for six years now. So you see what I see?"

"Yeah, I guess," I said. "They're a good family. Nice kids, a loving couple?"

"Yes, Amawi. Now. Look at that kite there that is stuck on that branch. See where I'm going with this? What do you see?"

"It's a black and blue kite, with a white tail, I guess? I don't know," I shrugged.

"Yes, true. But there's a ten-year-old boy who was flying that same kite one day in that field with his father. The wind was very strong that day and carried the kite away," he said.

"And it has been stuck there forever, and will be there up until the Apocalypse?" I suggested.

"Exactly," he said.

***

I woke up Sunday morning to a beep on my phone.

"Amawi, I need you to come over here now. Please," Puia said in a frantic voice.

My mind racing with a million possibilities, I jumped up, pulled on my t-shirt and jeans and ran over next door to Puia's apartment.

I rang the doorbell. No answer. I pressed it again.

Fifteen seconds passed. Come on.

I heard footsteps on the other side of the door. Puia looked ashen.

"Amawi, I don't know what happened. I woke up some five minutes ago and dad is not here and mom is on the floor, bruises on her face and blood on her lips. And I tried to wake her up but she wouldn't. I called the ambulance and they said they'd be here in ten minutes," he said. His words came out in a blur. His face had a sickly pallor.

"Puia, calm down, okay? It's okay. Where's Pa Mawia?"

"I don't know. He wasn't here when I got up. I called U Seni but she didn't pick up."

"Where's Nu Maawmi?"

He led me to the bedroom. She was lying on the floor.

Puia carried her in his arms and lay her on the bed. The morning was still dark and the curtains were drawn. I went into the bathroom, got a towel and soaked it in water.

Puia sat there on the bed, wiping her forehead with the cloth and it tore me into tiny bits to see the two of them like that. It just wasn't fair.

"Puia, everything will be okay. Your dad will come back and everything will be okay," I said. I didn't believe a word of what I'd said. I didn't believe things between his parents would be okay, because they had continued like that for too long. But I told him that they would be. He needed to believe that. There was nothing I could say that would make it better. I had to lie to comfort him, or at least tell him a half-truth.

But what if he held on to the hope that I had given him and nothing came of it? It would destroy him.

"That's just it, Amawi. I don't think I want him to come back."

His eyes were dark and heavy. He dialled his phone.

"Hello? U Sen? No, no, I'm fine. It's Mom. Dad...he beat her up," he said, almost choking on the words. "She's unconscious. No, I didn't see them. But I know it's him. He isn't here now. Okay, yeah, I called an ambulance. They'll be here soon. Yeah. Okay. Yeah, I'm good. Bye."

"She says she'll reach home today."

I nodded. "That's good."

We sat there in the silence. What on earth do you say in a situation like this?

"He said I don't belong here with them," he said, his voice hoarse, his tone angry.

"What?"

"Dad. He said I can't stay here with them. He knew about the drinking and the drugs. He told me I should leave or he would. Guess he decided to leave first."

The ambulance arrived a few minutes later.

"I'll go tell my parents," I told him.

"You don't have to come."

"No, that's okay. I'll come with you," I said.

I went inside. Anu and Apa were already up. "Where have you been, Amawi?" Anu asked.

"It's Nu Maawmi. She had an accident and now she's unconscious. They're taking her to the hospital. I'm going with them," I said, going upstairs to grab my backpack and not giving them time to argue.

I quickly grabbed my things, took a deep breath and ran back downstairs.

"Amawi, your mom and I discussed the matter, and we don't think that you should be going to the hospital, not right now. They're a bad family to be spending time with, honey. I know he's your friend but you have to know when to set the limits, sever your ties with people."

I couldn't believe this.

"His mom is sick, and I don't know what you think but he's a great person. He has some problems, but what about all of us?

What about you, Pa, when you were younger? You had the same issues."

"Quiet, Amawi," Anu scolded me. "He's trying to protect you. You know how sick you are. You shouldn't even be spending time with someone who is so emotionally unstable. You need to know when to protect yourself."

"I don't want you both to baby me like this," I said. I couldn't hold it in any longer. "I have to go, Nu, please?" I begged.

Anu and Apa looked at each other, contemplating what to do.

"No, Amawi. We've been through this before. You have exams tomorrow, you're sick right now. You can't go today," he said at last.

"I'm not sick," I said.

He waved my school notebook in his hand. "Your teacher gave this to us. Said we should read through some things that you had written here. He was worried."

"What? Pa, it's no big deal. I'll get through it. I'm fine!"

He stood firmly, his feet planted on the ground, like a tree taking root that no small wind could uproot. "Writing in a notebook that you think suicide is the only escape *is* a big deal. Amawi, listen to us. You can't go today. Any other day would have been fine, but today we are going to have a talk."

"Pa! Nu Maawmi got hit by Pa Mawia, okay? I need to go."

"What?!"

"Is that true, Amawi?" Anu asked. She looked sceptical, like I might have made up a lie to make them let me go. Why would I ever?

"Yes," I said.

"When?"

"He says maybe it was early this morning. He isn't sure himself."

"Oh my goodness," she said, gasping in shock. "Okay, honey. We'll take you to the hospital."

"I'd rather go in the ambulance with him."

"Are you sure?"

"Yes."

"Alright then."

The hospital was like all other hospitals—clean, white, and it smelled of disinfectant. I didn't like it. It reminded me of death, illness and pain. I had grown to associate the smell of hospitals with these three things and these three things only.

Puia and I followed his mom into the ER.

He looked awful. He walked up and down the waiting room, constantly rubbing his stubble. I told him to stop panicking. He said that he wasn't panicking and I told him that he was.

Anu and Apa sat beside me, looking worried sick. Anu pulled at the frayed edges of her sweater. Apa read a magazine but I could tell he couldn't focus.

After half an hour, Puia got tired and sat down beside me.

"Do you want to play rock, paper, scissors?" I asked him.

He breathed deeply. "Sure."

I pulled my feet up on the chair and turned towards him.

"Rock, paper, scissors," we both said. I won, then he won, then I won again, and again.

"Looks like luck isn't really on your side today," I said after he had lost for the fourth time.

"Nice observation," he said, his tone sad.

The small hand of the clock moved gradually towards nine. Hospitals sure could be a quiet place sometimes, mostly when there weren't many emergencies. I guess it's not really a place for bright and cheery conversations.

After some ten games, the doctor came back. "Puia, am I right?" he asked him.

"Yes," he said, getting up.

"Your mother is doing fine, Puia," he said, flashing a big grin. "She will get better in no time. The CT scan shows that she doesn't have any injury to her head, and the bruises will disappear in no time. We have put her in Room 54 for the time being. You can come and visit her."

"Thanks for taking care of her," Puia said.

"Son, these cases are quite common. If you have any problem, anything you need help with, feel free to approach the police or social workers," the doctor said, lowering his voice. "You need to get some rest now, come follow me to her room. We have a sofa and some food over there. And like I said, if you need anything." He looked Puia in the eye and patted him on the shoulders.

"Yes, doctor," Puia replied. Like he would ever listen to anyone.

He led us to her room. "We will monitor her condition for a few hours, just to be on the safe side. I suggest you stay here for the night. Insurance has got you covered. There's no reason to worry. It's better that we have doctors around her right now." With that he left us.

I sat down on the couch with Puia.

"You know what's so lame about all this?" He said. "That he would take out his anger on Mom. Her, of all people. She never did anything to him, ever. Yeah she wasn't the best mother I admit, but then she was always patient with him. And he was angry with me and he took it out on her. You know what he always said? He said, 'You should have raised him properly. It's your fault he's turned out a drunkard.' I'm not a drunkard."

"I know, Puia."

"This is so lame."

"It'll be okay." I hoped that it would be.

"I could've called the police before this happened. I shouldn't have waited. And now look at what he has done!"

He got up and walked towards his mom, sitting down in a chair beside her. He held her hand in his and at that moment, I could see him crying a million unshed tears.

U Seni arrived later that evening and the two of them hugged as she came into the room. U Seni was beautiful. She had Puia's eyes, long straight hair and was tall and gorgeous.

"Thank you for being here for our family, Amawi."

"It's no problem at all," I told her.

"This has been so hard on Puia. He really needs a friend like you now."

"I should probably leave. I hope Nu Maawmi gets better soon," I told them and made my way downstairs to my family.

On the drive back home, I saw a tiny black hole under my seat, its black nothingness enveloping me and wrapping its slimy arms around me. I kicked at it and it stayed still for a second, but started creeping up my skin again. Puia was inside it already. So was U Seni.

"Amawi, what do you want for dinner?" Anu said.

"We could eat out today. We don't have any leftovers at home," Apa said.

"That sounds good. Maybe some Chinese," I said, while I saw dark slime dripping from my jeans.

I forced my eyes shut and imagined an empty colourless space where a lilac chrysanthemum popped up, and then another one. I saw in a minute a pink rose wrapped in brown paper and white ribbons, and soon after a valley full of white lilies. I forced my eyes to see only these objects of wondrous beauty. My mind had to steer clear of all disheartening thoughts. I had to. It was how I had survived for the past two years, willing my thoughts away from its own designs. It did what it could to frighten me, leading me away from the present into a timeless space. An uninhabited, unexplored realm where the unthinkable happened and all I could see was what it wanted me to see.

Step Three of the Nature Lover's Guide to Survival: The Hills

Gather your books, a torch, a Bible, mosquito repellents, and a sleeping bag. Pack them all in a bag, taking care not to miss anything, and go to the hills of Mizoram. As you walk along lesser-known paths, think about how the breeze whispers in your ears words of encouragement and blows kisses on your cheeks.

Take a step back to consider how tall mountain grass sways in the wind like a Cheraw dancer, rolling along undulating cobbled paths ascending to the peak. Search for the aristocratic lavender of periwinkles and the sinful red of hibiscuses, and when you have found them, lose yourself in their sun-baked hues. Unpack when you find a shaded spot, away from the scorching heat of day. As you let your bag fall to the ground, stretch out your arms to embrace those flowering trees, the April Par and Chawnpui, and rest awhile in their comfort.

As the sun sets behind the hills, try to find marshmallows in the clouds. Imagine jumping in them and then diving to the bottom layer filled to overflowing with bunches of white wool and cottonseed. Picture finding in their dense white unimaginably delicate and soft dandelion fluffs and blow on them. Let them scatter in all directions, let the air carry them to the farthest reaches. Cover your hair with tender lace veils, stray strands sticking to your lipstick-stained teeth.

Spend the night gazing at the stars and take in the beauty of the amazing natural world that surrounds you. Rest awhile underneath the clear midnight sky, zigzag past the constellations, travel through the cosmos. Breathe.

SEVEN

I went to Puia's house some days later to visit Nu Maawmi. He answered the door with an out-of-character smile.

"Hey there, Amawi."

"Hey. How is Nu Maawmi doing?" I asked him. I could hear U Seni talking behind him.

"She's okay, I guess. I mean, she looks devastated but she's managing somehow." He looked behind him and called out, "Amawii's here. I'm going to the park with her."

"Okay. Don't be late," U Seni said.

He closed the door behind him, rolling his eyes and pulling on his sweatshirt.

"Let's go." He pulled me by the arm towards the park.

"Hey, what's wrong?" I asked him. He seemed on edge, like there were a billion things bugging his thoughts and clouding his judgment.

"I lost it today with her. She was bugging me about things and I told her to back off. I don't want them messing with me."

I didn't want to answer him. He would never have listened anyway, even if I tried to talk some sense into him. I could have told him they were right and that he should have stopped all this a long time ago, but then that would only have made things worse. He wouldn't change.

But then Puia was just Puia. He couldn't overhaul his life in a second, or do anything of the sort, I guess.

"You wanna talk about it?" I asked.

He shook his head no.

"Shame. Cos you take me out to the park like you want to meet up with me or whatever and you just stay shut."

He shot me a look.

"Listen, I don't need you to tell me what to do."

"Whatever." I kicked at some pebbles that lay near my feet and took a seat on a bench. "Maybe you should go to therapy. Talk to a professional. They'll know how to help."

He came and took a seat beside me. "I know how much you hate it there. You only go for the heck of it and because your parents make you go. It doesn't help much anyway."

"Don't you at least want to try?"

"Amawi, stop telling me to go to a stupid therapy session."

"It's not stupid."

"It is. Completely. Stupid."

I sighed. This conversation was pointless.

"Then don't go. It's your choice," I muttered.

"I don't even think I'll pass the exams."

"They'll understand even if you don't. Meet up with the principal or something and tell her about your mom."

"Yeah, I'll need to do that. But right now I just need a break from U Sen's whining about everything."

"It's like everyone around you is a nuisance, right? U Seni complains all the time about you, I tell you what to do, and your mom does too. Is that it, Puia? I can't seem to understand why you're acting like this."

"I spend time with you, don't I? Why do you say I'm mad at you, like how I am with my family?" he said. "I mean, you're a friend, that's all."

"Whatever, Puia. You're impossible."

Step Four of the Nature Lover's Guide to Survival: Root Bridges

Tiptoe along the rugged, intertwining root bridges of the forests of Meghalaya. Imagine a ballerina in tutus pirouetting along this rugged path, and pretend for a second that you're her. Imagine the twirls that you do mid-air, breathless, as the strong wind blows at you. Dance among these wonders of the natural world, and become the trees as you merge with their roots. Stand as tall as the Sequoia, a dusky, reddish bronze. Blossom every spring, shed your leaves every autumn, old dying things that have no value for you. Let new buds and leaves grow from old branches.

Be sure to walk and to keep on walking along these roots, never straying, never stopping except for a few seconds to replenish yourself. Be sure to have the right tools with you, and the right books to read under starlit skies. Carry a flute along for times when music is the only companion you have. Hum a tune as you walk along these mysterious roads. Remember that even in times of solitude you won't ever be alone. Creation sings praises with you.

When Puia and I were about five or so, we made a silly pact. We were in the same school, but in different sections. We had a half holiday that day and it was pouring heavily, like a war between dragons and baboons. I was standing near the gates under a small shed, waiting for it to stop. I was scared and hungry and started to cry.

Puia had seen me from his classroom and as his classmates ran down after the last bell, he called out to me. I remember we walked home from school together that day, sharing a small umbrella that his dad had bought for him. We reached home soaking wet and Anu dried us up in front of a small heater and made us some hot cocoa.

He made me swear that I would share my umbrella with him if it ever rained again and he didn't have one with him. I told him that I would and we even spat on it.

I had to be there for him. I had sworn that I would.

"Anyway, Amawi, my dad called me this morning…To tell me that he wasn't coming back and that I wasn't his son anymore... I had failed him. Can you believe that? *I* failed him. And to think that he called just to tell me that."

"Was he drunk? He may not have meant it."

"Yes, he was drunk. And yes, he's a moron. But that doesn't justify anything."

"I know it doesn't. I didn't say it did."

"It's not my fault, is it?" He said, smiling wanly at me.

"Of course it isn't, Puia. He's only trying to let you shoulder the blame for something he did. Don't believe a word of what he said. Show him what you're made of."

He laughed as I said that. "Even you don't believe what you just said."

"I do I swear. None of this is your fault. Did you tell U Seni?"

"Of course not. It will only worry her. Besides, she has to leave the day after tomorrow. Some seminar or something, I don't know."

"Things will get better," I said. I felt like I was lying.

I remembered the day we saw the three pigeons sitting on the rooftop. One had a wound on his left wing and Puia had pointed it out. He'd said that it looked like a wound from a sairawkherh. I got angry at the kid who must have pelted the stone at him.

Puia drifted off into his thoughts, an unreadable expression on his face. He looked dazed and inexplicably lost in a nightmare. The sky was bathed in pink light with wisps of stray clouds. There was a hint of black, warning us of imminent rain. I think he was wearing a navy blue jumper, or was it black, I can't recall, which had the name of some heavy metal band. It looked like a contradiction to the sky behind him. One with soft hues in an ordered realm, and the other a discordant jumble of deathly noise and emotion. I couldn't decide where I fit in. I gave up thinking about it and instead thought about the pigeon with damaged wings flying atop Aizawl and looking below him at the lights on the hilltops. I closed my eyes and pictured myself as a pigeon flying amidst sky lanterns on New Year's Eve and navigating past fireworks. Somehow I felt at home.

Step Five of the Nature Lover's Guide to Survival: Rainforests

You'll find all around you slugs and salamanders. Be careful not to get caught up worrying about the venom of snakes in places where it is unlikely that you will find any—that'll only slow you down. Be on the lookout for them only when there is a chance that they might be there, hiding in the tall grass, ready to strike at you in self-defence should you make a wrong move. Don't try to fight the inevitable. Rest in the heart of the forest, and as your best friend joins you, find shade and relief under the roots of a banyan. Let roots wrap around you. Derive from them nutrition. Tell your eyes to heal as the green envelops you. Immerse your whole self in it. Find in the rubber tree a different shade of green than you see on the climbing Lianas and ferns, and in the orchids new patterns and whole new shades of pinks and yellows. Train your mind to see and experience so much more of the beauty around you.

See how trees slow down in winters and shed their leaves to conserve water, and learn how you can shed whatever unnecessary weight that takes away from your wellbeing. Do what you should to heal. Search for God, call upon Him, and hear His answer.

As he dives into the river, hear how the water splashes around him, how it sprays onto your face, how the green water smells faintly of ripe avocadoes. Go into the river. Go underwater, search for electric eels. Gaze in amazement at how beautifully they've been thought out and created.

EIGHT

Four nights later, I woke up shaking and panicking and unable to breathe. I saw in my mind's eyes barbed wires encircling my throat and tightening their hold on me, and I saw myself tugging at them, trying to break free of them. There was nothing I could do to free myself. I fumbled with the wires trying to disentangle them but their hold on me became harder and tighter. I could only see dense fog around me, erasing the black wires from my sight until finally all I could see were my fingers, bloody and shaking, in the white fog.

I gasped for air, then gasped some more but it wasn't enough. I had to get up and walk out to my balcony to catch a breath of fresh air.

The night air was cool and calming, like always. I sat down on a mat, my legs curled up to my chest and rocked back and forth.

What would it feel like to die? Maybe wanting to die is much like dying itself, because the measure of pain would most probably be more or less the same.

The problems would be over. I wouldn't have to worry about anything. About hating on people. About hating on myself.

I rocked back and forth, back and forth. My breathing had returned to normal by then, so I went back to my room and switched on my bedside lamp, took out one of my books and read it for want of anything else to do, and then dozed off to sleep before I knew it.

Morning came, just like any other day. The day passed just like any other day, except I didn't feel quite normal. I felt queasy and sick to the pit of my stomach. It felt like my insides were being twisted like clothes in a laundry drier, and there was nothing I could do about it except wait for it to stop.

Maybe I should just let go, of everything. It would be better that way.

My parents won't have to worry about having a daughter who is always moody and depressed.

Maybe I should go.

Stupid stupid stupid why did I just say that?

Amawi, can't you see? You are a despicable nobody. Give it up already.

I'm not a nobody, I forced myself to think.

Maybe you should leave. Leave now before it's too late and you leave everything irreparably damaged.

Maybe, I said.

Then after two seconds, I thought about my parents who love me like their own lives.

Anu and Apa and I were having dinner when the queasy feeling came on again and I couldn't breathe, and the furniture and the food and my parents faded into the background and all I could do was sit there and gasp for air and try to breathe. Think, and gasp for air, again. But everything turned black in a matter of seconds.

I woke up to the familiar scent of sanitizers and crisp laundry and bedsheets.

I looked around me and there was a vase of roses on the table to my right, Apa half-asleep, sitting beside me and a nurse who was adjusting the tubes connected to the IV fluid that dripped slowly, drop by drop, and entered my blue veins. I had been there for I don't know how many hours, the fluid becoming one with me and all the cells that make up my body.

I looked at the wall clock as it struck twelve. It was light outside, so I assumed that it must be the day after.

"How is my little girl doing?" Apa asked me when he saw me waking up.

"I'm okay," I said. "How long have I been here?"

"Only for a while. You fainted at dinner, and your mom and I called an ambulance and got you here. The doctor says you had severe hypoglycaemia."

"Where's Anu?"

“She’s getting us some lunch. Your friends Faktei and Chhanchhani got you these roses. And Puia has been here all night. Amawi, why didn't you tell us you were sick?"

"I was okay a few days ago."

"But you weren't yesterday. Why won't you tell us about your problems? We're family. As family, we’re supposed to share things with each other."

“Maybe I don't want to talk about it, Pa."

“Alright, Amawi.” Apa looked years older right then. I felt like a jerk for having worried him. He left the room looking like a weight was hanging from his shoulders.

NINE

What if you had an epiphany about whatever you are dealing with and then you see the whole world through a new lens, and in a matter of seconds the world is bathed in rainbow colours. I always found that ridiculous and silly, a thing concocted for movies and for fairy tales. For me, it was more about having this constant struggle. It was never-ending. Sometimes I would see the hands again, in the dark of the night, covering my mouth, trying to stop my breath. I would panic for a second and then realize it's all gone now. He would follow me into my dreams, sometimes as often as three nights in a row, and I would wake up dazed. What I saw was the same—his hands gripping my arm and throwing my body onto the concrete floor. I shook the memory away and forced myself to see instead a field of red tulips and the sun setting behind them. It was near magical, the immediacy with which I felt undisturbed relief.

But my nerves started working up again the moment my peace was disrupted.

I say this because Puia started acting all strange around me.

He came over to my hospital room ten minutes later with drooping lids and dark bags around his eyes.

"Amawi, don't you ever do that to me again. You don't know how worried we were. If you're sick, you tell us. You don't keep it to yourself."

"I know, I know. I'm an idiot."

"I just had the worst time of my life. Don't you ever, ever fall sick again."

He had his Iron Maiden hoodie on, the one he wore the day we saw the family of pigeons sitting near the water tower. The day he told me his worst fears.

"What are you looking at?" He said.

"Huh? Oh, it's nothing."

"Is my hoodie a bit funny?" He smiled.

"No, of course not. It's nice."

"Yeah."

"Really."

"Okay, okay." He sat down on the couch beside me and tugged at the edges of his hoodie, then ran his fingers through his dark hair. "Amawi, I need to tell you something."

"Yeah? What is it?"

He stared at the vase of roses, maybe hoping to find the right words there, for a sentence to magically fall into place. Maybe he didn't find it because he sat still and quiet for the next ten seconds.

"What is it?" I asked again. I couldn't hold back a giggle.

"I'll tell you later," he said. "You look pretty today."

"Yeah?"

"Yeah."

"Thanks."

He ran his fingers through his tousled hair again, and for a fraction of a second, I saw a frantic sadness in his eyes.

“Amawi, do you ever just feel like giving up?”

“Many times, yes."

He frowned.

I could feel the hands of the clock crawling and ticking as time progressed.

“But you don’t understand. I try, okay? I try to be strong and brave and everything I’m not, but that’s just it. I’m not strong and brave. I’m a defect, some small insignificant fraction of a million bad things in this world,” he said. “My life is meaningless."

He was at it again. When would he ever get better?

“What makes you suddenly say that though?” I asked.

He wrung his hands together and picked at his cuticles.

“Arrgh. I don’t know okay? I don’t know.”

I continued to press him. “Tell me,” I said.

He stared out the window.

“I don’t want to sound angry when I say this, but please stop calling yourself all those things. Please try. Okay? You’re not insignificant. Just please stop saying that because it hurts everyone else too," I said, taking in a deep breath.

"I didn't think it would hurt you."

"Well, it does."

He frowned.

"Yeah. Sure."

"Stop."

He turned away from me, avoiding my eyes.

"Puia."

"I'm sorry I burst out. I messed up."

"It's fine."

After a pause:

"There's a tiger out by the woods today. And he was lapping water from a brook. You would never imagine tigers looking so peaceful," he said apologetically. His chin was resting on the bed.

"Thanks."

"This is what keeps you sane, isn't it? Your imagination. Nature and making it real on paper."

"It's what drives all that toxicity away. I like it. Remaking things. Reimagining the places I've been."

"That's good. You should keep at it if it helps you."

"Try it too."

"Of course I will."

"It'll work for you if it works for me."

"I know. I will… Your room smells of lavender."

"It must be the disinfectant."

"Huh."

"I like your hoodie. You were wearing it at the water tower."

"I'll give it to you." He smiled.

"It's two sizes too large for me."

"If you say so."

"Hey, Puia?"

"Yeah?"

"I'm praying that your worries don't bother you any longer. I want you to be happy."

"I know, Amawi."

I scattered petals on the floor and sprayed mists of perfume on the delicate things. I stepped on them with my bare toes and felt them squelch beneath my skin. They felt as smooth as paper.

"You remember three years ago when we went trekking in Reiek?"

"Yeah of course. Why?"

"There were dead leaves all along the trail and we stomped on them to hear them crunch under our feet. And guess what?"

"What?"

"The floor is flooded with petals now."

"Really? I don't see any," he said and laughed.

"I do. They're pink and lilac. Some are even blue."

"Huh. Anyways, I see them now."

"Do you like them?"

"They're lovely. The perfect shades."

"I told you."

Step Six of the Nature Lover's Guide to Survival: Coral Reefs

Dive into magnificently coloured coral reefs, take a dip in pristine waters where you find star-shaped amber corals and teal ones that look like bonsai trees. Explore this amazing underwater world. Let your curiosity guide you as you swim towards a gigantic blue rock-shaped coral that looks unlike anything you've ever seen, a half-coral, maybe half-stone, structure. The mystery is yours to unravel. Who knows what will come of it? You just might discover an ancient Atlantean civilisation down there as you swim farther below the surface. Discoveries only come to those who explore, and to explore is to reset your limits.

Sink your toes into the white sand as you bathe knee-deep in cool blue waters. Wade through the current, take time off as you bask in the warm summer sun, droplets of sweat running down your spine. Let the sticky ocean breeze send grains of sand onto your tongue, and see how different it feels from anything else you've ever felt. How new, how exhilarating it is.

Listen to seashells that tell stories from ages ago, stories carved in their every nook and cranny. Stories told in song of the oceans that they travelled and the storms that they braved. Search the beaches for a message in a bottle. Be the listener and the audience that the writer never had. Maybe never wanted to have. Explore the different stories that people and objects hold. Who knows what you may find when you redefine your boundaries and take the time to let curiosity run wild like a paper kite without strings.

TEN

"Amawi, I need to talk to you," Puia said, coming into my house one evening.

He pulled me by the arm and out through the door.

"Puia, where are you taking me?" I shouted. "I need to be inside. Anu and Apa are at work."

"I don't care about that. I need to talk to you," he said.

"Okay, can't we talk here?"

"No. I need to get away from this place."

He pulled me into his car and turned on the ignition as he slid into the driver's seat. He was drunk. I could tell by the alcohol in his breath. A shiver of panic ran through me.

"Puia, calm down, okay? Stop the car and we can walk around the park or something if you want to talk."

He didn't listen. The car was already out on the streets, and Puia was rushing his way past the buildings, past the familiar cafes and delis where we used to hang out. I was terrified.

"Puia, you don't have to do this. Pull over!"

"No."

Just like him to never listen to a word I say. I told myself I should pray. I hadn't done that in a while.

I closed my eyes and whispered a short prayer. Two sentences. That was as much as I could manage.

But then there was no magic wand that I could wave to make it better. I was still riding shotgun next to my best friend who was now whizzing past the streets driving drunk.

I guess when you have so much fear, you just sort of become numb to everything. I didn't fear that we would crash. I didn't even fear that we would get pulled over. The only thing I was concerned about was keeping Puia sane so that we could escape this nightmare unscathed.

"Then what is it you wanted to talk to me about?" I asked him.

"It's not important anymore, Amawi."

I bubbled with rage when he said that.

"Then why would you drive me out, drunk, just to tell me that you have nothing to say to me? What's your problem?"

He kept on driving, staring straight ahead but it looked like his mind was not even on the road. He buzzed past traffic posts and honked at every car in front of us. He almost ran into a dog that was sleeping on the roadside. There were no traffic policemen around to stop him. Everything around me was a haze.

I took out my phone. “I’m going to call the police if you don’t stop now.” I threatened. That didn’t really help because it only made him drive a lot faster than before.

“Call anyone you want, Amawi. I don’t care anymore.”

“Puia, stop it! You’re going to get us killed. Don’t you care if we died?” I yelled.

“That’s just it, Amawi. You don’t trust me. You have never noticed, have you?”

“Noticed what, Puia?”

“All of this.”

“I don’t really care about that right now. Pull over and we’ll talk.”

“No. I won’t.”

“Damn it, Puia. You can be so stubborn sometimes. Okay, you know what? What is it you wanted to say to me? Say it now.” We might as well get this conversation over with. If I knew Puia, he wasn’t going to stop until he got what he wanted.

“You really haven’t noticed, have you?” he looked like a stone had just hit him in the gut.

“Noticed what?” I asked. I was starting to get annoyed with his evasive answers.

He scoffed at me. I didn’t want to ask again, so I let it go. I didn’t want him driving me around town drunk, saying that he needed to talk to me just to scoff at me when I asked him what he wanted to tell me.

I looked out the window. My heart was thumping wildly in my chest, my pulse rising. I wiped my now sweaty hands on my jeans. This wasn’t going well.

“And to think that I trusted you.” He looked hurt and scared even under the influence of all that alcohol. I couldn’t help but feel bad for him.

“Puia, what’s going on?” I asked again.

“Do you even care?” He asked me, not answering my question.

"Puia!"

He glanced over at me, his eyes dark and wild. He looked furious.

"I need a break from everything. Let's get away from everything. Just for today."

When he remained silent and averted his gaze to the road in front of us, I asked him, “Why?”

He released his foot from the accelerator by a fraction. We slowed down. We were now well into the heart of town.

“Let's just go. I don't need a reason. I just need to get away from it all."

"Puia."

"You will never know, will you?"

"Know what?"

"Never mind. You never get anything."

"Get what? What are you trying to say?"

"I said never mind."

"Fine."

We sped through Chanmari past a dim street light.

I shifted uncomfortably in my seat. I looked at the speedometer. We were now going at sixty kilometres an hour.

"Dad came home yesterday," he said, staring straight ahead as he drove. His expression was grim and ice-cold. I was always scared of him when he acted like this.

When we were younger and I was bullied at school, he wore that expression as he told the other kids to back off, grabbed my bag and lunch box and walked me home. He walked me right up to my doorstep, knocked on the door, and told Anu and Apa what had happened. He wore that same cold stare then. I knew he was standing up for me, but it scared me even then.

It still scared me now.

"What happened?"

"He came for his things. He told mom he didn't want to see her again, he told me he wanted me out of his life, and that he doesn't even think of me as his son."

He slammed his hands on the steering wheel and I jumped in my seat.

"Calm down, Puia. Everything's fine. Everything will be okay."

"Will it? I lost my dad…"

I said, "I'm still here."

"I love you, Amawi," he stomped on the accelerator. "But you never get it."

"Puia, slow down. Please."

His mind was somewhere else, oblivious to every word I was saying.

"Why didn't you ever tell me?" I asked him.

"Why would my feelings matter anyway, Amawi? They're just a nonsensical network of neurotransmitters and hormones and electrical signals. Feelings are science. Feelings don't count," he said. Then he glanced toward me, looking me deep in the eye. I looked at his and they seemed sad. "At least mine don't. Your feelings matter. Your happiness matters more to me than mine does."

I didn't know what to say. I kept quiet.

"So you agree? My feelings don't matter?" he asked me.

"I didn't say that, Puia. Of course they matter. I'm sorry."

"I hate this, Amawi. I HATE THIS."

"Puia, you're drunk."

"I'm not."

He stepped on the accelerator.

"Stop!"

He didn't.

With a vague certainty, I had a premonition of impending death.

I didn't know what I felt then, because the car tumbled as he tried to swerve to avoid another car coming from the left and we rolled onto the road. I heard frantic shouting and the sound of people calling for help. The next thing I knew the world was turning into a meaningless void.

Everything became a meaningless void.

ELEVEN

I heard doctors shouting, calling the nurses to hurry into the ER. Pale white lights surrounded me.

I saw my mother bending down towards me and crying. I could feel her hand soft like a feather on my forehead and a sharp pain everywhere else.

I drifted off again.

I woke up after I don't know how many hours. The hospital room was clean and white, with a window covered with a floral curtain to my left. I saw Apa sleeping on the couch to my right, covered in a small blanket, a newspaper lying on his chest.

"Apa," I said, but then I realized that my head throbbed with pain when I tried to speak, so I didn't say anything more. My right arm was covered in a big cast.

"Amawi," he said, getting up and walking over to me. "How are you feeling?"

"I'm okay," I managed to say. "How's Puia? Is he okay?"

His lips pursed and his eyes grim, he said, "He's still unconscious, Amawi."

I closed my eyes.

This was all my fault. I should have stopped him from going out. I should have taken the keys from him.

"Will he be alright?"

"I don't really know. He lost a lot of blood."

I nodded.

"They had to give you a couple of stitches here and there. And you broke your arm in three places. But you'll be fine."

"How long have I been here?" I asked.

"Only for a day, dear," he said. "Let me go tell your mom, okay?"

I nodded again, my head throbbing from the effort.

Then the events of the day the accident happened came flooding back to me.

If his dad hadn't said that to him, he wouldn't have taken the car out just to run away from his fears. He would have been okay.

I just wanted so badly for him to be okay.

When Anu came, she told me that the doctors said he was in critical condition. They didn't know when he would wake up, if he ever did. He had had a serious blow to the brain. His internal organs were severely damaged.

When things like this happen, I get nervous and I have panic attacks and I think that the whole world has let loose all its misfortunes on me. I wonder if there's a single good thing in my life, and I curse at everyone and everything around me.

Not this time. This time was different.

This time I needed to be stronger than that.

I guess when you're at the depths of despair, you come out stronger than you had the courage to assume you are. I guess it's because you get tired of feeling sick, or the world has done enough to tire out your weary bones, but whichever way it goes, I think that it is true. When you feel you can go on no longer, you come out stronger. It's odd logic, I know, but trust me it's true.

That evening, my friends came to visit. They entered the stark hospital room with a bouquet of beautiful and fragrant lilies.

"Amawi, we were so worried," Faktei said, placing her hand on mine.

"I'm fine," I said, forcing a smile. "My head hurts a bit but I'm okay."

She smiled. "That's such a relief. You need to rest though. You look awful."

"No, I'm fine. It's just this migraine," I said. I closed my eyes.

I could see black and white all around me in my mind's eye. Black space with white and green lights and red fluorescent dots everywhere.

"You'll get better in no time," John said. "We'll be here if you need anything."

"Okay."

And before I knew it I drifted off.

They must have left soon after because I found the lilies in a vase when I woke up with a get well soon note from them and my father sitting down on the couch reading a book.

Being in a hospital feels like you're being walked to your funeral. It's no joke. It feels like all these doctors and nurses are fighting all these illnesses for you and there's nothing you can do but to let them fight your fight. It's embarrassing that you can't even fend for yourself. Once you get hospitalized, you're a sick bag of puke and IVs and blood transfusions. You find out that you actually need help from other people.

And you thought you could always do things on your own, like you're superhuman or something. Trust me, once you come face to face with danger, you'll realize that you're a lot more like porcelain. At least your physical body is. Inside you can be iron and steel but outside you can crack in an instant. Life is fragile I guess.

Bones are fragile. So are limbs and brains. Your brain will go into a deep sleep for forever and you'll need all these tanks of oxygen and IVs to support your frail body. If you're lucky, you'll wake up. If not, your family will have to call relatives and tell them about the situation.

I only see that in the movies, these actors putting on tears for family who are in hospitals, battling pain and death, but when it happens in real life it hurts a whole lot more. Your future, your whole life, is in jeopardy.

But maybe Puia would wake up.

He would. I was sure he would.

There was no other option.

Many survive accidents far worse than this, I had heard, unless the fates decided to be cruel to them. They carry on with their mundane lives, and even the most ordinary day-to-day events start to assume profundity. They start going to church or maybe to a temple or a mosque, but whatever religion they believe in, they always speak of how God has saved them and given them a new-found hope and a new beginning. Like their misfortunes were a wake-up call to go to grander heights or something.

Puia would also wake up and he'd see how his mistakes led him to a near-death experience and he would go to school and after that he would go to college. I'd tell him that it's okay that he got me into an accident, and maybe I'd ask him about what he had said about loving me. Whether it was just drunk talk or whether he had meant it. Things would be okay.

This was how things were supposed to be. There was absolutely no other way.

I calmed down after that. Because I knew that he would wake up, heal, and everything would be alright, like they had always been.

I said a silent prayer of thanks for that.

TWELVE

When I was about nine, I would spend all my summer days at Puia's house since my parents were always at work. Nu Maawmi would make all these momos and shakes for us. There was a time when I was going through the stage of wanting to become an undercover agent with all these cool cars and gadgets and cameras. I talked Puia into becoming a secret agent just like me. He said he wanted to fight Russia and maybe become James Bond one day (the inherent effect of years of watching Spy Kids and James Bond movies, if you ask me).

We'd grabbed a large bedspread and lugged it into his dark closet. It was musty and smelled like it hadn't seen sunlight for days. Clothes and shoes crowded the small space. We barely fit into the makeshift tent.

"Amawi, I need you to go undercover for me. Here, put on your disguise," he had said, grabbing a large can of black poster paint and opening it. He dipped in two fingers, as much as would fit, into the can and smeared paint all over my face.

"Done, sergeant," he said. "Romania needs you to save President Nabokov. He is being held captive by Russian Forces and they've put him in a cave full of snakes and rats. He'll get bitten by a snake if you don't hurry."

"Yes sir!" I said with ten times more energy than if someone had just offered to take me to Willy Wonka's chocolate factory.

I pretended to put on my special gear and gadgets and what not silly ideas I had about what spies wear on their missions.

"Hurry, Agent," he prodded.

"Wait, I'm stuck," I said. I couldn't seem to put on my black invisibility t-shirt.

"Hurry!" he said again.

I was struggling into my t-shirt when I heard a loud thud on the front door. It was his father.

Puia froze. He stared wide-eyed at the door to his bedroom. Even at that age I could tell that he was scared.

"What are you doing sitting in front of the TV? Get to work! Women like you were made to take care of the house, not watch silly Soap Operas!" His father shouted. He was most definitely drunk.

"It's only one hour. I need a little rest too," his mother said.

"Do you think you have the right to answer back?" he said and then we heard a loud shriek, and Puia rushed out of the tent, and out through the door to his room. I followed him into the living room where his father was hitting Nu Maawmi.

U Seni was sitting on the dining chair as pale as a full moon and shivering.

Puia lunged at his father and bit his arms. He thrust wildly at him and beat him with all his might.

"Don't do that to my mother! Don't do that to my mother! Don't do that to my mother!" He repeated again and again.

He was sobbing and weeping as he hit his father, who eventually sat down to have another shot. Guess he didn't have the courage to fight back someone like Puia.

His father probably knew about the accident. It was all over the local papers. U Seni must have called him too.

But he didn't come. He didn't come to see if his son was okay.

I always thought that the guy didn't have much love in him. He was selfish. Nothing more could be said.

A day later, I could get up and walk about. The migraines didn't hurt as much although my entire body ached from the force of the impact. My arm was covered in a big cast that made it uncomfortable to eat and use the bathroom, but I was getting better I guess.

I walked over to the ICU where Puia was. He was now a pale skinny boy with tubes and wires surrounding him, a bundle of tubes that kept him alive and electrical signals and beeps that indicated whether he was okay or not, the only medium through which we could communicate.

One look at that boy and I knew that everything would be okay. He was going to wake up any day now and he would go home to his mother and U Seni. This nightmarish disaster would be over then. I knew it would.

Ancient civilizations such as the Greeks blamed natural calamities on the alignment of the planets. Even the word disaster comes from the Middle French *desastre*, which comes from the Old Italian *disastro*. This is derived from a Greek word that means 'bad star'.

So once the stars and planets aligned, things would get better. I wasn't into astrology, but I hoped beyond hope that this time it was true.

I guess when you lack the courage to admit your faults and mistakes, you start to turn the blame onto other things, things that couldn't possibly have had anything to do with it. It is easier that way.

It's funny how even the most common words are grounded in some ancient belief—in this case an irrational pseudo-science that makes extraordinarily outrageous claims and generalizations about someone's character.

Puia and I had always scoffed at our horoscopes. He used to wonder how anyone could believe those weird predictions.

"I'd rather live today without any worry about tomorrow. If someone prophesied to me that I was gonna die five days later, I'd probably spend the whole of the remaining hours of my life in perpetual fear. Who would want to live their last days worrying, right?" he had said one day. I remember it was some three years back. We were at a small fair at our school and one stall had hired an astrologer. Kids flocked to him to have their palms read or whatever shenanigans they do to predict the future.

"Not me," I agreed.

Gosh I missed talking to him.

But it's alright, I told myself. You'll be chatting like old times in just a few days. Be patient.

His mom sat down on the couch next to his bed and stared into the empty space in front of her. Her expression was listless. She snapped out of what must have been agonising conversations with herself as I walked over to her and sat down beside her.

"Amawi, Puia always likes to be around you. You should come every day to visit him. He needs company. He's always lonely, my little boy. He misses his father," she said as she gazed at nothing in particular. "Talk to him about what you're studying at school. If it's from you, he might start to develop an interest in his lessons. He's always looked up to you, you know. You've always been a close friend to him."

She wrung her hands together and hugged herself. Hospitals can be a cold place. The bitter smell of disinfectant gets associated with the smell of sickness and mortality and all you can feel here is apathy and disengagement. A sort of numbness that overpowers all your senses until you become languid and unfeeling. Some people say that doctors are cold. I guess spending all your waking hours in a place like this *makes* you cold. It's not like they're inherently unsympathetic and unkind.

"I will, Nu Maawm," I said. I didn't know what else to say. What could I say to console her? Nothing I could do would help much. Sitting there with her and offering her some company would have to suffice I guess.

"Whenever he came home from school he would rush into the kitchen where I was cooking and taste the food. He was always the first to taste my cooking, and he would tell me if it wasn't salty or if it was not sweet enough. He has a sweet tooth so I couldn't really trust his judgment when he said it wasn't sweet, but I would add just a spoonful of sugar for his sake. He is such a good boy, isn't he?" A tear trickled down her cheek.

"Yes, he's a good person. He's fun to hang out with and he'll do anything he can to make you smile," I said, trying to call all of his virtues to mind. "And he's funny too, and smart and caring. He's brave and courageous. He will do all that he can to stand up for the people he cares about."

I rambled on and on, glossing over all of his weaknesses and sugar-coating the bitter parts of his life.

A nurse walked into the ICU and asked us to leave for a few hours. They needed to conduct some tests.

"Pi Maawm, you should get some rest," the nurse said. "There are empty beds near the waiting room. You'll see a sign that says Nurses' Station to the right of the entrance. Tell them Debbie sent you there." She was dressed in a green shirt and white pants and had her hair tied up in a ponytail. She looked like she was in her mid-twenties, but she had dark circles under her eyes. She was the one that needed rest, I thought.

"Yes, thank you," Nu Maawmi said.

Chhanchhani was waiting outside, sitting cross-legged on a chair and tapping her fingers on her knee. She rushed to meet us as soon as she saw us leaving the ICU and gave me a hug.

"Glad to see you're all in one piece," she said. "Hello, Nu Maawm."

"Yeah, a piece and three smaller pieces," I said, referring to my arm.

"Yes! I need to sign your cast," she joked.

Nu Maawmi looked pale as she greeted Chhanchhani. Her initial fear and anger had faded into moroseness. When you're in an elevated emotional state, be it negative or positive, it's hard as hell to fall asleep. You toss and turn in bed, close your eyes, count sheep, take pills, anything you can do to escape the nightmare. But sleep always eludes you when you need it most. Once you fall asleep, you won't wake up even if someone were to blow a whistle near your ear.

Chhanchhani and I left the waiting area to return to my room. She sat down on the couch, flipping through the pages of a fashion magazine.

"Oh, this dress is so cute," she said. I was relieved that she wasn't talking about the accident and that she was being her old Fashionista self. She held up the magazine for me to see. An anorexic model in a navy blue and white striped skater dress adorned the cover page.

I agreed that it was. I was relieved that she didn't ask me about the accident.

"Amawi, can I ask you something?" she said after a while.

"Sure." Like I had a choice.

"What happened? In the car?" she looked at me questioningly. She had strong instincts—she must have known somehow that something was not right.

I decided to tell her. She wouldn't let it go if I didn't. I felt a huge weight lift off my chest as I related every detail to her. It was a relief that she came right when it hurt most.

Right then I was some insignificant detail in the universe, some mass of dark matter that could not be used for anything good. I was undetectable. I wasn't stardust. I didn't make up the bodies of comets and meteors. I was anything but that.

"It's not your fault, Amawi. You couldn't have stopped him," she said. "It's not Puia's fault either. It's not anyone's fault because we are all just people and we all need to be forgiven. Don't be so hard on yourself."

I was silent.

"He said that he loved you?" She asked me.

"Yes. He'd been trying to tell me, I just couldn't see it. And I call myself his friend," I said.

"I should have seen that too, Amawi. I should have noticed how he had changed over the months."

A temporary silence filled the air between us. It was overwhelming to think that words were always so empty, and that they could do so little. If I had a magic word for disasters such as this, I would think words hold value. If only they could bring about change and turn things around.

***

I left the hospital after two days. Anu and Apa and I went for a walk.

The hot afternoon sun burned the grass dry, and dozens of cicadas hummed to the beat of our footsteps as we walked around the warm and lazy park. Things felt a lot like lifelessness itself, and even all that humming and buzzing couldn't do much to animate the dead surroundings. Since the summer afternoon was bordering on thirty degrees, most people stayed in their homes. Guess they were a lot smarter than we were to come out only at dusk for their shopping and evening walks. Only the headstrong and foolish seek to brave summer afternoons (and many more arduous situations). Some people are wise enough to stay away.

I had been praying for Puia to recover but he hadn't shown any sign of life for days now. Even an hour can seem like days. His whole being was dependent on machines now. Tubes and electrical wires and tank after tank of oxygen. Who knew that human life could be reduced to such low depths?

I visited him in the hospital that evening.

I walked into the ICU and Nu Maawmi wasn't there. Neither was U Seni.

I sat down next to him. He looked peaceful, sleeping on the hospital bed like he was in a deep sleep. Like a small child.

"Hey, Puia," I said. I felt silly talking to him. "How are you doing?"

No answer from him. Not even the twitch of a muscle.

"Right. Stupid question, I know. You'd probably be telling me that I need to act like a normal person with a normal IQ right now." I laughed. Laughing alone at your own jokes can make you feel vaguely idiotic.

"We're lonely without your silly jokes and your crude remarks. We miss you. We all do."

I waited for him to wake up. Ten seconds passed. The heart monitor beeped on in a steady rhythm, softly, like the whisper of moonlight in a dark sky. Nurses shuffled into the room to check on their patients.

Come to think of it, we're all nearing our end, slowly by slowly, every day. Some people have fifty years before they die and some have fifty seconds. You never know how long you've got. I guess we should live out our best days like they were our last. You just never know when you might have an accident, or the last time you'll hear someone's voice.

"Puia?" I whispered next to his ear. Maybe then he would hear me, without the space between us.

Nothing.

His hand lay cold and lifeless by his side. There was an IV tube stuck into his veins. His hair lay dishevelled on his forehead, some strands covering his eyes, his olive skin pale and yellow.

I reached for his hand, then hesitated. I placed my arm on the bed.

I reached for it again, and this time I held it, encircling my fingers around his palm. It was cool and damp.

"Puia. Can you hear me?"

I felt the nurses observing me out of the corner of their eyes, contemplating this cruel sight with a mixture of sadness and pity. I felt sick.

"Pui, did you mean what you said? In the car?"

The incident came flooding back to me.

"I'm sorry I didn't understand before. I wasn't listening to you."

The heart monitor beeped on, oblivious to every word I was saying. His heart was alive and well. Maybe the heart guides our emotional states. Maybe it isn't just some organ full of cardiac muscles after all. His heart was alive. It knew what I said, so he would feel something when I told him this secret, one that I realized not too long ago. His emotions would get aroused and he would wake up. A futile and foolish thought.

I decided to say it anyway.

"Puia, I love you too."

I waited for a minute.

"I loved you when we were kids playing silly games with your dogs, and when you carried that Pikachu umbrella for me, and when you stood up for your mom and your sister, and that time when I was sick and you let me cheat off your answer papers. I love you. I do. There's so much to lose, Pui. Wake up please. Please." I cried for him to hear me and answer me.

He didn't.

There was no response from him.

Just his short, regular breathing. The beeping of the machines. The nurses and doctors. Shuffling footsteps. If I listened closely, I could even hear the slow drip of the IV. But not the sound I wanted to hear most.

Step Seven of the Nature Lover's Guide to Survival: Snow-capped Mountains

Mountains getting uprooted around you and being cast into the sea by faith as small as a mustard seed. Gusts of wind blowing at you, blocks of ice bursting into showers of snowflakes falling on your face. I catch a falling flake on my tongue and it sends a shiver down my spine. It thrills me to think that the same piece of matter that makes icebergs could be this minuscule, this small.

Mountains look smaller from a distance. Sometimes, it's like they don't even exist. All I can see is the candlelight at the top, faint at times but burning nonetheless in the foggiest of storms, and the occasional flower bed at lower altitudes, bright with lilacs and pinks and amber yellows peeping from a field of green. Craggy mountains emerge from the dense greenery, rising skywards into thinning clouds. They appear impenetrable from down below, what with their jagged surfaces and steep cliffs. It takes courage to take a step towards them, but a step taken is a journey half completed.

THIRTEEN

I got a call from U Seni the next day. She told me that Puia's condition was getting worse. I rushed to the hospital and reached at exactly 2:16 p.m. The hospital clock read 2:15 p.m.

I reached the floor where the ICU was. U Seni and Nu Maawmi were there looking ashen and thin. They had spent days here and it had taken its toll on them.

"Amawi, you came," U Seni said.

"It'll be okay," I tried to reassure them. I sat down on the hard wooden chairs and watched the small hand of the clock reach three, then four.

Still no news of Puia.

John and Faktei and Chhanchhani arrived soon after. They sat down next to me. There was pin-drop silence. There wasn't much to say. I got up, restless, and paced back and forth along the corridor. John sat silently, legs spread apart and hands to his chin. Faktei looked worried—she constantly picked at her cuticles. Chhanchhani stared into space, her eyes red. I observed the passage of time and bit my nails.

Anu and Apa arrived after work. Anu ran over to Puia's mother, who had emerged from the ICU, and hugged her. Adults know how to show solidarity in situations like these.

"Guys I'm going for a walk," Faktei said and got up. John and Chhanchhani and I followed her.

We strolled along the main building of the hospital. There were lots of sick people here. People in wheelchairs. Some on stretchers. The dying with forty years ahead of them taking care of the dying with only a day left. The world has lots of sick people. It is one of the things it is made of. The thought made me sick.

"Gosh I just needed to get away from all that," Faktei said. "It's so depressing."

We didn't answer her. There was no need to affirm her thoughts. We all knew that it was depressing beyond words.

"Plus all these sick people everywhere," she continued. "Hospitals should have more colour. It's like all those neutral shades are saying, 'Welcome to the land of boredom and death! Enjoy your stay here!'"

We let her ramble on. She always did so when she was panicking.

We returned to the waiting room at 6:36 p.m.

Soon after, a doctor wearing a grey uniform walked out of the ICU. He came over towards us. He said something to Puia's mom. She turned deathly pale and mumbled something inaudible and thanked him.

She turned to U Seni who had been standing beside her the whole time the doctor was there. They held each other and cried.

People say that every day is a beautiful day. Everything in this world is gay and sunny and cheerful. Reality check: well, it isn't. It's dark and dreary, like the moon is collapsing in the dark of the night or something. People always tell you that there's always a brand new day. A new chance. A new start. Tomorrow will be a better day.

Well what if your last days are your worst days? What if you don't get a tomorrow like you had hoped you would? What if your dreams of eternity have been cut short?

I couldn't cry for Puia. My lungs and my chest felt heavy and I was numb. I was emotionless.

Faktei continually rubbed her eyes with her handkerchief and John sat stunned. No one could talk. There was nothing to be said.

It was over.

I lay awake in bed. It was already 4:11 a.m. The red lights of my bedside clock showed that it was. I could hear the soft tinkle of the wind chimes near the door to my balcony. The small LED lights glowed in the darkness of the room. The wind blew into the space around me and the posters rustled above my bed.

My chest was still heavy and I felt strangely detached from everything. I wasn't myself. I was someone else living in the body of a sixteen-year-old girl.

All this was an illusion and things would be okay soon. I knew they would.

I took in a deep breath but as soon as I did so, I had a pressing need to take in another deeper breath, and another after that. My breathing became heavy and I sat up straight, telling myself to breathe.

People tell you that death is an inescapable part of life and that the dead are at peace now. They lived a sad existence here on earth, and now they are at rest. They are asleep and are oblivious to pain and sorrow. We their loved ones and family should be happy for them instead.

They don't tell you that it's okay to feel like you want to die too. They say that that's a selfish thing to wish for. That it's cowardly. Most people don't get what it's like to feel so low that you'd do anything to lessen your pain. About wanting to know the freedom there is in not feeling anymore.

When someone close to you dies, each breath that you take reminds you of your inescapable mortality. You want each intake of oxygen to be your last and final one here on Earth. You wouldn't care much if it was anyhow. What did it matter?

I stood up and walked over to the desolate space outside. Everything around me was sombre black and blue. The buildings formed a silhouette against the milky sky, while pale clouds roamed across the vast expanse.

Maybe with your final breath, you would feel better.

Maybe the pain would end.

I didn't have the courage to do it though.

Or maybe I was braver than I'd thought. I didn't know which.

Whatever the case, a new sun would rise tomorrow and bring with it a new day. It would be a new chance at a new life. Or at least that's what all the blessed would say. They don't know how bad things can get.

I stood there in the cool air of the morning and watched the sun rise to my right. It came up slowly, a golden orange globe of fire and light.

The world around me was collapsing and everything else was oblivious to it and unsympathetic. People would go to work today and school would start in a few weeks. Everything would be routine and mundane, but never the same again.

I felt like I was suffocating, but I didn't try to breathe. I let myself feel it, that pain, as I stood there, my hands on the railing and the wind blowing on my face and the sun rising higher, and everything continuing just as it had for centuries before me. Before the earth ever saw us wasted youth.

Maybe the world had seen too many dead people now to be sympathetic towards them. It had seen people for thousands of years, and within that span billions of lives had been lost. New lives are lost every day. Maybe some people just didn't count. The whole world would have mourned for someone famous, someone influential, but Puia's life didn't matter. He was just a teen who drank and did drugs. He caused his own death because of drunk driving. Shame on him, they would say.

I kicked at the pots and I wanted to shout but my throat was tight and I couldn't say a word.

I cried hysterically. It felt like I was getting delirious.

The world can be biased. It favours the rich and famous, people that are in a position to better its state of existence.

It just doesn't notice young insignificant people like Puia.

FOURTEEN

Step Eight of the Nature Lover's Guide to Survival: Volcanic Plateaus

You see around you waves of hardened lava from a volcano that erupted years ago. It is miles long but if you cross it, you'll reach a field of daisies and sunflowers. You need to take that first step, but it looks scorching hot and the flames near the top haven't died. Fresh lava spews out from the crater. Harness all your strength, whisper a silent prayer and as the soles of your shoe land on a piece of hardened lava, you will feel the solid ground. You jump on it and stomp on it with all your might to test its strength, because your brain is crazy foggy from sleep deprivation, and it may surprise you that it is cool and hard. You hadn't imagined the lava would be this solid. All you saw on TV were flowing rivers of molten lava consuming everything in their path and leaving behind no traces of life.

Take sips of water every now and then as you trek through this dark landmass. When you rest at night, look up at the stars and see how lovely the night sky can be in the absence of city lights. Count them on your fingers, and be awestruck as you realize just how many lights in the sky there are in the wilderness.

As you reach your destination after a lonesome journey, look for the first signs of life around you. Bend down towards the ground. You will find a single daisy with shrivelled leaves blossoming in this deserted place. Take a few more steps and you will see more sunflowers popping up from the black lava. Soon you will cross the lava fields and reach a field in full bloom. Rest awhile here. Let it calm your anxious thoughts and soothe your troubled heart.

***

School started two weeks later. Who would have imagined that we would finally reach our last year of schooling? Our board exams would greet us a few months later. There were tons of assignments to be done and books to be read, projects and all the other unimportant stuff that you're forced to do in schools. Our class teacher was this bald guy named Paul Chaitanya. He taught us Home Science. No one really listened to his classes, but he gave us good tips on how to write our exams.

There were now fifty-three students in our class, not fifty-four, and an empty chair right behind mine. It felt strange seeing it unoccupied. Last year, a tall, lanky and handsome boy used to sit there. That boy had gone on to do greater things. School was too silly for him anyway. That's what I wanted to believe and what I would tell myself.

I still woke up every day expecting Puia to return. I wanted to see him bursting into my room again and talking to me about his life and his family. I needed to hear his voice again. I needed to see him one last time and ask him so many questions that had gone unanswered.

I walked home with Faktei on the first day of school. I had always gone home with Puia.

When someone that you love dies, it feels like things could never be worse. People tell you to move on and that your wounds will one day heal, but the cold fact is that there will always be that part of your brain that loves that person and does not permit you to forget until your brain dies and your heart stops pumping blood. You can't escape even in your sleep. They show up in your dreams whether you want them to or not.

There were these times when I felt desperately lonely and sad. Then these feelings would leave me all of a sudden and I would be laughing at someone's joke without actually hearing anything that they had said.

I didn't hear anything that anyone said most times.

I would have given anything to not feel a thing right now.

I wanted apathy. I wanted to be emotionless.

Feeling too much for too long can get to you after some time I guess.

"Amawi, is it okay if I come over? I seriously need to talk to someone right now," Faktei said.

I hated to talk about this. What was there to talk about? There was nothing that could be done now.

"Sure," I answered.

We walked into the living room and sat down to watch some TV. I curled up on the couch and grabbed a bag of chips and started munching on them.

"I can't seem to stop dreaming about him," she said. "It's always the same dream, night after night. I see the three of us walking together, and talking about something silly and laughing. Then it's just the two of us and I see Puia there standing behind us. He says something but I can't hear him so I run over to him but I can never reach him. And then I bolt up from my bed and it's early in the morning, around 3:00 a.m. I can't sleep after that. It happens every night."

"I miss him too. I think about him all the time."

"This is so difficult, Amawi."

I held my arms tight around me and said that it was. We were merely stating the obvious. I did not want to talk about this.

"I went to his grave the other day," she said.

"I don't have the courage to do that. It's like he's not even there, like he's somewhere playing a cruel practical joke on all of us and laughing at his own jokes."

"It doesn't feel real."

It didn't feel real because the young are not supposed to die. They are meant to live out their lives to a ripe old age and have kids with their partners and then have lots of grandchildren and great-grandchildren. They're supposed to make chhangban for their grandkids when they come to visit and maybe tell them stories of Chhurbura, sometimes teach them to knit, I don't know. But they weren't supposed to die at seventeen.

"Do you think his family is okay?" she said after a pause.

"Not really. They can't be. It's impossible to be," I said.

"His father didn't come to the hospital."

"He must still be feeling hostile."

It felt like we were talking about a stranger.

"But Puia is his own son, Amawi," Faktei said in a tone that I had never heard from her before.

I remained silent. Words didn't suffice in this situation. They were mere sounds, rearrangements of letters. They didn't seem like enough.

"I'm just so angry," she said. "I'm angry at him too, and that makes me feel guilty because he's no longer with us and I don't wanna be angry at him for anything. He shouldn't have had anything to drink before he went to the car. What on earth was he thinking?"

A talk show was airing on TV, something about a celebrity caught with illegal drugs.

I only heard bits of what Faktei was saying.

There's this theory in Psychology known as the Gate Control Theory. Pain signals do not reach the brain straight away from an injured tissue or site of damage. They need to pass through these things called 'gates' which are located in the spinal cord. These gates can allow the signals to pass through or they can stop them. So you may be stung by a bee or something and you won't feel a thing unless these neurological gates are opened.

I guess the same thing goes for emotional pain—you feel only what you want to feel. All the rest of the emotions? You block them out. It was quite simple really.

FIFTEEN

Step Nine of the Nature Lover's Guide to Survival: Cities

In the city I find a tapestry of emotions—happiness, clouded, left tattered in storms, held together by sublime faith and courage. A drop of red on a plain white sheet. A desk on which a white piece of paper is pasted, printed on which is the random roll number of a student in his twenties, the paper now torn. A few interesting points to jot down in an otherwise monotonous lecture. All that I hear is the whirring of fans above me and the occasional gust of wind that sends the leaves outside rustling and dancing in this humid August air.

But in the city, there I find a tapestry of emotions.

A budding romance. The endearing sight of an eighty-year-old woman waiting for her grandson at his school bus stop. A man jogging with his wife of twenty years. Best friends since five, going out for ice cream. Colleagues unwinding at a small tea stall during their thirty-minute lunch break, sharing bits and pieces of their lives, leaving a few things hidden in between diary covers. A young woman walking her eight-year-old dog, and him running around her in circles and sniffing at the grass and marking his territory wherever he hasn't done so before, and a young genius whose life hangs on a precarious balance, receiving a call from a friend from middle school. A mother helping her dyslexic son with his homework and teaching him to find music in the discord. A homeless man sharing his food with a malnourished dog.

In the cities and towns, you'll find polka-dotted skirts twirling under a clear blue sky and buskers strumming their guitars and singing as though for the whole city, even when no one as much as glances in their direction. People running to catch the last bus home, like shadows with heavy shopping bags slipping into dimly-lit buses in the twilight, to go home.

***

One week later I found a frayed notebook in my drawer. I had never seen it before. A sticky note pasted on it had my name on it. It was in Puia's handwriting. I flipped through the pages and saw diary entries starting from a year ago.

An entry that was dated 30th October of the previous year read:

"There is a black space there in the distance, and it is advancing closer and closer. It will inevitably reach me and consume me. I cannot escape it because I have become enticed enough to succumb to its deathly claws. I only hope that I will be forgiven. That is my sole relief now."

I read it again. His life must have hurt like death to be inspired to write these lines.

I put the diary down, not wanting to feel like I was trespassing, but after a moment's thought I decided that Puia must have wanted me to read it.

"I will not admit to Amawii that this is what I feel for her—this feeling, an emotion that somehow makes me believe that all the wrong in the world can be righted again. Her absence has become unbearable, her presence a reminder of how unattainable she is. I had vowed that I will not burden her with my lame confessions, but promises are easier to break than to keep."

I hugged the book close to my chest, as though it were Puia reincarnated or something and I cried. How did it end up here? Why hadn't I noticed it before the accident? Why?

I sat down on the bench near the marshes and ran into the rainforest where I saw him diving into the river. I thought of all the things we could have done together, and all the things that could have been. I should have paid more attention to him after he told me what he was feeling. I wanted to tell him that it is okay to hurt, and that it doesn't mean that it is the end. I wanted him to know that and nothing else. Nothing else that would tell him otherwise.

There is this entry from Puia's diary that he had written some months back:

"Life is a splendid entity—it will present you with the most phenomenal people that have ever walked this tiny globe. It will

bring you an abundance of love and faith, of the things that matter most. Life is a wonderful and generous benefactor.

But people are not infallible and people hurt one another. We bring despair to the ones closest to us. I have always wondered, often angrily, why that is the case. It's a part of life in a fallen world with fallen people I guess. We wage war on innocent nations. We murder children and tear families apart with little remorse. We drop bombs on whole cities and call it self-defence.

Our fallen world contains a lot of imperfect citizens who live imperfect lives. Our lives are intertwined and we bring hurt and pain to each other. But one thing that I can say with reasonable certainty is that no matter the situation, it gets better in the end. The past may not have been so great, and you may be ruminating on events that have passed, trying to clean up the broken bits.

Let me tell you though. It's less about cleaning up the wreckage and more about rebuilding the ship. So start over, have fun, don't take things too seriously, love like you have never loved before. Take this advice from someone who has made tremendously idiotic decisions. As long as you have today, remember that you are blessed beyond comprehension."

We love you, Puia. We all do.

Step Ten of the Nature Lover's Guide to Survival: Cherry Blossom Lanes

A forest full of blooms, where pink hues carpet the muddy path. The soles of your shoes land softly on the baby pink earth, and you dive into a silken sapphire sea that fills your lungs to saturation with cherry blossoms. You become the sea for a split second as your mouth fills with fallen petals, as it enters your living cells. A mutation in your DNA, and now you are part human, part flora. Millions of petals weigh you down and you shake them off to get a whiff of fresh air.

Your feet grow a bundle of roots that merge with the earth, spreading to the rocks beneath. You stand firm in the midst of this sapphire forest. You look behind you and you see a woman draped in ethereal white, and it's the woman you knew before you knew this world. The nurturer who gave you life through the strongest connecting factor known to exist in us, the first physical bond between mother and child—cut at birth, but still present as an intangible, inexplicable force that draws you to her for all your needs.

With her is the bearded lion of the savannahs, the warrior of his pack and guardian of his kind. Together they stand behind you as blossoms dance in the wind and make a tiny whirlpool. You get caught in it and it's magical to see your body flying in the wind like fallen petals. You feel magical in the wind.

GLOSSARY OF MIZO WORDS AND PHRASES

Alu papawr	A popular snack made with potatoes and papad
Chhangban	A delicacy made with pounded sticky rice
Chhurbura	A character in Mizo folklore, known for his comical actions which border on lunacy
Chinai	Limestone
Em	A large basket made by weaving bamboo
Kuhva	Paan
Mautam	A cyclic ecological phenomenon that occurs once every 48-50 years; the flowering of a species of bamboo, *Melocanna baccifera*, causes a rat population boom, which further causes famine
Puan	A woven piece of clothing traditionally worn around the chest; now worn by wrapping it around the waist
Sairawkherh	Slingshot
Tuikhur	Well

Note:

Anu, Apa, Api and Apu are terms of endearment meaning mom, dad, grandma and grandpa respectively.

ACKNOWLEDGMENTS

I started writing this book while in college, and completed it during the final semester of my master's programme. It would have sat unread for a lifetime and longer if not for the encouragement and support of my family, especially my mom and my dad. Thank you for believing in me. Thank you, Nu Tetei, for reading my drafts.

Thank you to Lalropuii for her guidance, especially during the writing of the first few versions. Thanks to Zomuansangi, friend and Beta-reader, Angela, Juliet, Lalnunpuii, Vanlalawmpuii, Zohlimpuii, Grace, and Mary. Thanks to Vinay Kumar, Christie Rachel Saji, Ishanee Sarmah and Jahnavi Gupta for everything.

www.ingramcontent.com/pod-product-compliance
Lightning Source LLC
Chambersburg PA
CBHW050020170726
48282CB00025B/478
* 9 7 8 8 1 9 9 0 6 5 1 9 2 *